The Sword of Justice ...

What fairly stopped the breath in Wentworth's throat was the monstrous idol which filled one end of the chamber. Wentworth had seen various manifestations of Siva in a hundred Indies temples, but no such nightmare monster as this could be conceived. In general outline, the figure was conventional, but the face held a malignancy that stirred revulsion and rage deep in the soul. Even more horrible were the six visible arms of the god. As if they, too, were deadly snakes, they twined in sinuous convolutions and the bronze hands plucked and plucked again at the altar beneath its knees!

Men's hands closed on Wentworth's arms, and he felt the ropes sliced from his wrists! For a moment, he thought some hidden friend had done it, but all too soon he recognized his error. The men who held Justice McTavish hurled him to the floor and ripped the clothing from his aged body. Within a space of seconds, he had been laid upon that awful altar and the hands...the hands of Siva were upon him!

Wentworth understood then why his hands had been freed and a shout of rage beat against his clenched teeth. Four of the hands of Siva had fastened upon McTavish, each by a separate wrist or ankle, and were lifting the sagging body. It seemed a gentle thing at first, the way in which those four hands raised the aged justice—but only at first. Then the arms bowed out, and McTavish's body no longer sagged. It was stretched out rigidly in the torture rack of those bronze hands. Stringy muscles bulged hideously in the man's body and a weak moan was squeezed from his bitten lips.

"In this way," lifted the clear, changing voice ... "shall the enemies of the Sword ever perish!"

Richard Wentworth had reached Washington in response to a newspaper column's personal, "In the name of democratic humanity, come to Washington before September 9..." He knew that this marked only the beginning of a yogi-ridden dictator's reign. Behind a welter of machine guns and storm troops moved the Cobra, striking at the nation's very chief—and the SPIDER was face-to-face with the strangest battle ever fought by man!

©**1998 Pulp Adventures, Inc.**
All Rights Reserved. No part of this publication
may be reproduced or transmitted in any form.

THANK YOU:
Mark Alvarado, Joel Frieman, Rick Hall,
Frank Hamilton, Don Hutchison, Phil Nelson

MACHINE GUNS OVER THE WHITE HOUSE
A Pulp Adventures, Inc. Book / published by arrangement with
Argosy Communications, Inc.

PUBLISHING HISTORY
Originally published in THE SPIDER Magazine, September 1937
Pulp Adventures, Inc. edition published December 1998
First Printing • December 1998 • 1,000 copies

Front Cover illustration: John Newton Howitt
Interior Illustrations: John Fleming Gould
Back Cover Illustration: Franklyn E. Hamilton

MACHINE GUNS OVER THE WHITE HOUSE, by Grant Stockbridge, from THE SPIDER Magazine, September 1937. TM and Copyright © 1937 by Popular Publications, Inc. Copyright renewed © 1965 and assigned to Argosy Communications, Inc. All Rights Reserved. Reprinted by arrangement with Argosy Communications, Inc.

DEATH SIGNS THE PAYROLL, by Frank Gruber, from THE SPIDER Magazine, August 1937. Copyright © 1937 by Popular Publications, Inc. Copyright renewed © 1965 and assigned to Argosy Communications, Inc. All Rights Reserved. Reprinted by arrangement with Argosy Communications, Inc.

"The Web" ©1998 by Don Hutchison. All Rights Reserved. Printed by arrangement with the author.

"THE SPIDER" and "THE SPIDER—MASTER OF MEN!" and its distinctive logo and symbolism and all related elements are trademarks and are the property of Argosy Communications, Inc. All Rights Reserved.

PULP ADVENTURES, INC.
P.O. Box 64
Bordentown, NJ 08505
Tel. 609-291-5050

http://members.aol.com/pulpress/index.html

email: pulpress@aol.com

Rich Harvey: Publisher

Cat Jaster: President

ISBN: 1-891729-05-5

PULP ADVENTURES and PULP ADVENTURES PRESS are trademarks and are the property of Pulp Adventures, Inc. Its distinctive symbol is based upon an existing trademark owned by Argosy Communications, Inc. All Rights Reserved.

Printed in USA.

THE WEB

Conducted for the Spider
~ by Don Hutchison ~

MASTER OF MEN! Was there ever a magazine with a cover legend more unusual? Or more fitting?

Handsome playboy by day, grotesquely-garbed horror by night, the *Spider* waged war on the ungodly with the frenzied passion of an Old Testament avenger. To the dispossessed of the dirty thirties he was heaven's messenger with a gun. While despair gripped the nation, when jobs disappeared, and even nature itself seemed to turn against America, the *Spider's* wrath vanquished criminal conspiracies as vast and as frightening as the Great Depression itself.

Alone, injured, perhaps near death, his beloved city in flames or ruins around him, the law, the public, and even his loved ones turned against him, the *Spider* soldiered on. For he was The Master of Men. And for The Master of Men there was no surcease, no rest.

FRANKLY, the Spider stories were as preposterous as anything any cranked-up pulp writer ever put to paper...And yet, with all their illogic and over-the-top melodrama, those of us who read them then remember them still. They are recalled not just because of their unique mix of action, fantasy, and sensationalism but, surprisingly, because of their human warmth and passion. Alone among pulp heroes, Richard Wentworth —"The Master of Men"— triumphed with messianic fortitude through agonies of personal loss, injury, betrayal, and blood sacrifice.

We now know that a half-dozen authors contributed to the Spider saga. But there was only one true "Grant Stockbridge," and his name was Norvell Wordsworth Page. It was Page who took over the series with the third issue and who found in a heretofore conventional pulp hero a perfect conduit to express his own deeply-held beliefs regarding idealism, faith, and duty...even if those concepts were expressed through science-fictional nightmares of monumental carnage.

Page's approach to the pulp hero formula was to exaggerate the sheer magnitude of his villains' crimes and their utter disregard for human life as a contrast to his hero's nobility of purpose. In his mad universe, the Spider's Manhattan was a city under monthly siege by fiends as bent as boomerangs, its major landmarks imperiled by flames, bombs, or death rays, with tens of thousands—perhaps millions—of innocent citizens threatened or destroyed by disease, drugs, or the ruthless incursions of subhuman hordes.

As his vivid imaginations sped recklessly past the borders of reality, Page's compounded horrors moved beyond the Big Apple into state-wide and even nation-wide settings. It seemed only a matter of time before the nation's capital itself might fall before his Apocalyptic vision. That happened in *Machine Guns Over the White House* in September of 1937.

INTERESTINGLY, this was only the second Spider story written by Page following his mysterious disappearance from the series in 1936. In it, glimpses of the real world—the one his readers actually lived in—creep into the *Spider's* febrile nether world. Only four years before, Adolph Hitler had been proclaimed Chancellor of Germany and his brown-shirted minions shouted *"Heil! Heil Hitler!"* In the *Spider's* parallel universe an American demagogue surrounds himself with green-uniformed troopers shouting *"Hail Chief! Hail! Hail!"*

Machine Guns Over the White House presaged a trilogy of *Spider* novels published a year later (*The City That Paid To Die, The Spider At Bay, Scourge Of The Black Legions*) in which New York state falls under the totalitarian rule of a Nazi-like empire replete with concentration camps and armies of fearsome Black Police. In the later series, parallels to Hitler's evil Reichstag were even more obvious, although still distorted through the lens of pulp hero convention. Clearly the *Spider* stories were not meant to be taken seriously. There were disposable entertainments written at white-hot heat by a master pro who no doubt amused himself by stretching everything to near snapping point. If he chose to add subliminal messages about love, trust, loyalty, and even the odd political admonition, that was but icing on the fictional cake.

Machine Guns Over the White House is simply glorious, outrageous pulp. The year is 1937. A Congress of crooks controls the nation's capital. "Storm Troopers of Justice" strut the city streets, torching homes and roasting citizens. Hindu cults and turbaned knife-throwers patrol the Potomac. Sacrifices are made to Siva, "evil god of the cult of the Cobra's Fangs." And the President of the United States (presumably F.D.R. himself) is threatened with death by public hanging. Only Richard Wentworth—one shoulder broken and lungs bullet-punctured—stands in the way of total anarchy. To the enemies of his beloved nation he delivers steel-jacketed death. And on their pallid foreheads he stamps a vermillion seal of tensed hairy legs and poison fangs—the *Spider's* weird symbol of swift and ruthless justice.

It is pure pulp melodrama and pure Norvell Page.

Enjoy.

DON HUTCHISON is an award-winning author and editor who has been writing about the pulp magazines for over thirty years. He has published four books on the subject, including **The Great Pulp Heroes***, now in its second printing. His latest book,* **The Scarlet Riders***, focuses on Royal Canadian Mounted Police stories from the pulp magazines.*

Machine Guns Over the White House

By
NORVELL PAGE
(writing as "Grant Stockbridge")

Cover Painting by
JOHN NEWTON HOWITT

Story Illustrations by
JOHN FLEMING GOULD

The SPIDER Created by
HARRY STEEGER

~ also ~

"Death Signs the Payroll"
By FRANK GRUBER

"Machine Guns Over the White House" was originally published in THE SPIDER Magazine, September 1937

THIS SEAL GUARANTEES YOU

THE BEST REPRINT FICTION!

Pulp Adventures Press • Bordentown, NJ

MACHINE GUNS OVER

Before the horrified eyes of the Senate's jammed galleries, that revered Senator died by his own hand. And Richard Wentworth, who had reached Washington in response to the newspaper agony column's personal, "In the name of democratic humanity, come to Washington before September 9..." knew that this marked only the beginning of a yogi-ridden dictator's reign. Behind that welter of machine guns and storm troops moved the Cobra, striking at the nation's very chief—and the SPIDER was face-to-face with the strangest battle ever fought by man!

THE WHITE HOUSE

A Feature-Length Spider Novel By
NORVELL PAGE
~ Writing as "Grant Stockbridge" ~

The underworld was intimidating justice with cold-blooded ruthlessness.

CHAPTER ONE
The Sword Of Justice

FROM THE time when the press services of the nation half-humorously dubbed him the Boy Wonder to the day when they respectfully accorded Roger Holme his own title–the Sword of Justice—precisely twelve months elapsed; twelve of the most fantastic months in all America's mad history. As if to celebrate that anniversary fittingly, the local Holme-for-President club lynched the mayor of Indianois City.

The local boys had just heard Senator Roger Holme speak and he had told them the mayor was a crook. So they hanged the mayor very carefully in chains to the portico of his home. They heaped his furniture beneath his feet and touched it off with gasoline. His wife and daughter heard him screaming for quite a while...

When interviewed by the press, Senator Roger Holme said: "It is regrettable. I had already boarded the plane for Washington when it happened and apparently the boys got a little too enthusiastic. But, after all—the mayor *was* a crook!"

He made that statement at Hoover Airport in Washington, his marvelously flexible and musical voice booming out to the throng that had gathered, even so early in the day, to welcome him—such a crowd as greeted Holme everywhere—and the people screamed their approval.

The same copy of the New York *Times* which told of these events bore on its third page a four-line personal advertisement in what is known as the agony column. It read:

SPIDER — In the name of democratic humanity, come to Washington before September 9, or it will be too late. Dare not say more.

Cicero e pluribus unus

So the people in their need cried out to the one servant who never failed them—to the man who, furtive as the nocturnal-creature whose name he bore, must ever work in the shadows in peril of the law and of criminals he ceaselessly fought in humanity's name. It was proof of his greatness that he never counted the cost to himself. It was warranty of his astuteness that hours before the paper bearing this appeal was on the streets, the *Spider* already had left for Washington.

This man who to the secret few was the *Spider* but who bore before the world the distinguished name of Richard Wentworth, stood waiting against the wall of a hangar when Senator Roger Holme's plane swooped out of the sky at Hoover Airport. He heard Holme's callous comment on the lynching, and anger began to eat its slow course through his veins. All about him, men cheered and whooped their approval. One of them whirled on Wentworth.

"You didn't cheer!" he accused hoarsely. "You didn't cheer the Sword of Justice."

"No, I didn't." Wentworth's brows were lifted quizzically. What madmen these followers of Holme were, that the mere failure of a bystander to cheer could stir them so! "No," he repeated. "Senator Holme has done some great work, but what happened in Indianois City last night is—*anarchy!*"

With a shout of anger, the man flung both clenched fists above his head. Meeting the quiet gaze of Richard Wentworth, he did not strike. Instead, he swung about and raised a harsh alarm!

"This crook is against the senator!" he yelled. "He called him an anarchist!"

INSTANTLY, the white faces of the crowd focused on him. A mutter that became a roar swelled from them. Men began to run toward Wentworth, waving their fists. Wentworth's eyes flashed keenly about. He was not afraid, but he did not underestimate the temper of this nascent mob. They were dangerous. Lord, what power this Holme wielded over his followers! Grimly, Wentworth decided that he had done well to come to Washington. He stood lightly balanced on both feet, not aggressive, but competently ready as the shouting people became a packed mob before him. On the outskirts, women's voices lifted shrilly.

"Lynch him!" one cried. "*Lynch* the dirty crook!"

Wentworth's face was entirely serious. He

had come to Washington, to the airport, to make his own estimate of Roger Holme. From afar, he had grasped the waxing power of this man, and he had to know—the *Spider* must always know!—how Holme would use his power. For today, September 9, the Senate would vote on a bill which could make this man a mighty force for evil or good. Wentworth lifted his resonant voice clearly.

"Senator Holme!" he called. "Senator Holme! Some more of your boys are becoming too enthusiastic!"

The mob's shouts rose in a snarl, but Wentworth's words reached Senator Holme at the door of his limousine. Holme turned, his bared bushy head lifted in the attitude of challenge that was characteristic of him. The early sunlight enlarged him, stretched his shadow like a great sword upon the ground as he peered toward where Wentworth stood, backed to the hangar wall, ringed in by the howling mob.

IT WAS a dangerous experiment Wentworth had launched. If his appeal to Holme was ignored, the mob would hurl itself upon him— but he would have made his estimate of Holme's character! It was characteristic of the Spider that, regardless of personal peril, he had deliberately chosen this way to discover how Holme would use his power. On Holme's actions, Wentworth was increasingly convinced, hinged not only his own life, but some part of the nation's future. Already there were Holme-for-President clubs, and his following was tremendous...If Wentworth could have known then about the agonized appeal to the Spider, and what lay behind it, his fears might have driven him to immediate frantic action!

There, beside his limousine, Holme still hesitated. With him stood a lean, stooped figure: Elias Godlove, his secretary and chief investigator of graft through whose revelations Holme had risen to his present stature. During that wait, Wentworth's confident bearing did not falter. His was ever a commanding presence. In another, more gallant age, he would have risen spontaneously to kingship with that erect almost arrogant carriage, the piercingly magnetic quality of his intelligence. He was a born master of men. Behind his quietness, his mind was questing sharply. If Holme failed to heed his call...

Abruptly, Senator Roger Holme was striding across the hard-packed earth of the airport. The mob fell silent and opened a broad avenue through which he advanced until he and Wentworth stood within two yards of each other. Even then, Holme did not at first speak. News reels and the radio had brought something of this man's personality to Wentworth, but nothing could have prepared him for the really terrific impact of the man himself.

Youth, vibrant strength and energy, magnetism, intelligence—all of these qualities he had, together with an intensely dramatic appearance enhanced by that challenging lift of the head beneath its bristling mop of thick, fiery hair. Yet even that formidable sum did not explain to Wentworth the man's meteoric rise. There was mystery here. A year ago, Holme had been a newspaper reporter elevated to mayor of a midwestern city after his sensational expose of political corruption. Today, he was a national figure whom the Senate might endow with extraordinary powers!

"You called me," Holme said finally, his voice rich and full as always.

Wentworth bowed slightly, studying eyes quizzically on Holme's face.

"Quite," he said. "One of your adherents challenged my failure to cheer for you, Senator. I'm afraid my explanation excited him. I said that what happened last night in Indianois City was anarchy. Rather than have some one hurt in the melee that was threatening, I called to you."

An angry mutter ran through the crowd, but the gaze of the two men held and slowly Senator Holme smiled—with a boyishness that contrasted oddly with his usual, almost pompous, gravity.

"Thank you," he said. "I never wish the innocent to suffer. May I offer you a lift to the city, Mr..."

"Richard Wentworth."

"Richard Wentworth!" Holme's eyes kindled. "I know of you. I think we may find something very much in common!"

Wentworth bowed, and the plastic mob cheered as the two men strode side by side toward Holme's waiting car. A girl with a hotly flushed face leaned out of the mob to shout in incoherent admiration. A man swung both arms in the air and commanded a cheer for the "Sword of Justice."

At the door of his car, Holme abruptly faced Wentworth with the air of a man startled by a sudden memory.

"Come to my office at four o'clock," he ordered abruptly in a tone of dismissal. He handed Wentworth a card on which he had scribbled rapidly. "This will admit you. I really want to talk to you."

He jumped into his car and was whisked away, but not before Wentworth had a glimpse of the interior. There was only one person there beside Senator Roger Holme, a woman with a still, pale face. It was only an impression and then Holme was gone while Wentworth stared after him, between anger and amusement. The man gave himself almost royal airs...

A hand touched Wentworth's arm and he turned coldly, to peer into the dour, stern face of Holme's secretary, Elias Godlove. For a moment, Godlove's eyes rested on his—gray chill eyes that burned with a strangely fanatic fire. And Wentworth felt a tautening of every muscle in his body, a bitter wariness creep into his brain. Danger, these things shrilled in Wentworth's heart—*Danger!*

Godlove's voice was nasal, rasping, "This car, please. Step right in here."

He gestured toward a second sedan and Wentworth saw that three men ringed him in, their gaze pinned alertly on his every movement. To all intents, he was a prisoner! A slight, reckless smile stirred Wentworth's lips. He bowed punctiliously.

"You are too kind," he murmured and climbed into the car.

HE ALLOWED himself to be crowded against the left-hand side, so that his right arm would be cramped by the man next to him—by Elias Godlove. The car ripped out the parking space into the highway at terrific speed. A siren whimpered beneath the hood and traffic skittered from their path.

Between narrowed lids, Wentworth's eyes remained alert, but his body seemed utterly relaxed. The smile lingered on his lips as he considered this Boy Wonder who tomorrow might become one of the nation's most powerful men. Though he felt an instinctive liking for Holme, who could grin so boyishly at another's quiet courage, he knew that here was menace, the darker because he could not put his finger upon it. This smiling, boyish man had inspired a mob to anarchy and murder! And he was too well served.

Wentworth turned casually toward Godlove. "Permit me to point out," he murmured above the rush of the wind, "that we are not taking the most direct route to the Hotel Marquette where I am staying."

Godlove's coldly burning eyes rested sardonically on him, then his face went abruptly rigid. It had not bothered Wentworth that his right arm was crowded against his side. His hands could serve him equally well when it came to drawing one of the twin automatics that nestled in clip holsters beneath his arms. His left hand presented the automatic almost casually against Godlove's stomach. Fury writhed in Godlove's eyes, but it was not apparent in his voice.

"Drive to the Marquette," he called to the chauffeur. He turned back to Wentworth. "I expected you to abuse our hospitality. You will not call on the Sword this afternoon."

"Your hospitality," Wentworth told him lightly, "is a bit too pressing. As to Holme, I will suit myself about calling. It appears to me, Godlove, that the investigator could stand a little investigation if I make myself quite clear!"

A cold, tight smile only sharpened the angles of Godlove's face. He turned away and did not speak again, even when Wentworth alighted at the Marquette and stood facing the car, hand resting significantly on his coat lapel, until it drew away. He swung about then and went swiftly into the hotel.

The clerk called to him, "New York has phoned four times, sir, in the last hour!"

A frown contracted Wentworth's forehead. "I'll take the call in my room," he said shortly. "Call them back at once."

NEW YORK calling. That meant...Nita Van Sloan! Alone among her sex, she shared the perilous secrets of the Spider, this woman whom Wentworth loved. If she were calling so urgently, it meant some fresh danger. When the phone bell rang, Wentworth sprang to the instrument and within moments Nita was telling him swiftly of the frantic appeal to him that had appeared in the Times. As Wentworth copied it down, word for word, his face drew into stern lines.

SPIDER — In the name of democratic humanity, come to Washington before September 9 —

"That's today," Wentworth said crisply, "and it's the date the Senate votes on the bill to create the office of Secretary of Audit and Finance, which would go to Holme, of course. He has strength enough to compel his own appointment. And the bill would give him enormous powers to search for graft and crookedness. *Democratic humanity*—the advertiser foresees a threat to democracy. That's probably a hint at dictatorship. *Dare not say more*—sounds as if violence threatened, perhaps criminal violence, and that idea is borne out by the signature, *Cicero*.

"You'll remember from your history that in the Roman Senate, Cicero exposed a criminal conspiracy by another senator named Cataline to overthrow the government. Our Cicero is probably in the Senate and the rest of the signature *e pluribus unus*—apparently means that he's one of many who fear the consequences, yet who dare not resist. If this is a true statement of circumstances..."

Wentworth's voice died, and Nita interposed a quick question. Wentworth's words grew slower, "Yes, I realize it's difficult to understand how exposure of dishonesty could be a menace, but if Holme himself were crooked, he could use his power to destroy enemies, to make himself supreme. Look what happened in Indianois City last night! Then, if..."

Wentworth had been subconsciously aware of some changes in the situation in his room. It was no more definite than that at first, but his acutely trained senses never tricked him. When he realized that a draft struck now across his shoulders where before there had been none, he acted with the swiftness of thought. Whipping his body forward, he thrust back his chair violently. His chair tripped on the rug, upset and struck against something directly behind Wentworth which had not been there brief moments before when he sat down to the desk to phone! He heard a man gasp out a single harsh oath and Wentworth sprawled sideways to the floor. His right hand flicked beneath his coat lapel and as he rolled to his back, a heavy automatic sprang into his fist.

The scene that met his eyes might have startled a less alert man into immobility—and accomplished his death. Reeling backward from the blow of the chair was a man who, Wentworth saw incredulously, had the swarthy skin and green turban of an East Indian! In his right hand, the man gripped by the neck a writhing snake. The jaws were open and Wentworth recognized that blunt head, those lethal fangs. A *krait!* One of the deadliest snakes in the world and Wentworth knew that those fangs had been within inches of his unprotected throat when he had acted!

Even as Wentworth stared with widening eyes, the Hindu lost his balance and pitched backward. As he fell, he hurled the deadly snake directly at Wentworth's face.

CHAPTER TWO
Death On The Floor

IT IS given to few men to think with absolute and lightning clarity in life-and-death emergencies. In Wentworth that trait had been deliberately developed through continuous training amid a lifetime of peril. Wentworth realized, as almost no one else facing such horror could have, that the krait could not hurt him except by an accidental contact of the fangs at the instant its hurled body struck him. He realized with equal certainty that, within a half second after the snake landed where Wentworth lay flat on his back on the floor, it could coil and strike again and again.

A lesser man might have tried to dodge away—and would have died. Wentworth might have risked a shot with a fair chance of hitting the snake and flinging it away with the driving power of lead. But if he missed—he died! As surely as the *Spider's* alert brain clicked to the only solution, so deftly Wentworth's left hand shot out and closed over the cold, powerful body in midair. There was no time to gauge the catch to a nicety and his hand gripped the deadly snake near the tail, leaving the dangling head free to strike and kill! But Wentworth gave the *krait* no chance for that. His left hand cut a swift circle in the air and he hurled the snake back the way it had come!

So quickly had the entire thing happened that the Hindu's body was just striking the floor when Wentworth flung the snake away. In an instant, Wentworth was on his feet, gun ready.

"Lie there, motionless!" Wentworth ordered, his voice slicing incisively across the room.

The Hindu glared defiance. He lay helpless on the floor, hand gripping the knife he had barely drawn. The snake, flung violently against the farther wall, was writhing in its death throes.

"Now drop the knife!"

For a moment, the man seemed about to attack in the face of that deadly steady gun, then defiance went out of him. With a resigned spreading of his hands, the Hindu dropped the knife. A grim smile brushed Wentworth's lips. He took a step backward and scooped up the telephone with his left hand.

"Everything is quite all right, Nita," he said quietly. "My interpretation of the message was correct, too. Criminal violence threatens!"

His eyes quested over the delicate features of the Hindu, took in the hands, as shapely as a woman's. "No, no dear," he told Nita. "Nothing to worry about now, a Rajput tried to kill me, but he's out of the fight now. Yes, a *Rajput*.* Strange for one of his high caste to turn assassin...No, Nita, you stay in New York. Send Ram Singh to me by the first plane. Tell him to go to the usual place and I'll communicate." If this were to be a battle against the Orient, his Sikh body servant might serve him well indeed! His voice sobered. "Guard yourself, my dear. God alone knows where this will end."

WHEN Wentworth hung up, he crossed at once to the snake and seized it behind the head. By pressure of thumb and forefinger, he opened the mouth, thrust it close to the face of the Hindu on the floor, while he still covered the man with his automatic.

"Now, thou pig of no caste," Wentworth spoke in a fluent and idiomatic Hindustani. "Thou wilt speak with the tongue of truth!"

The Rajput's lips curved in a slow smile. With a movement as quick as a snake's, the captive Hindu deliberately jerked up his head—and tried to drive the venom-laden fangs of the *Krait* into his face! Wentworth sprang erect, and the Rajput was in instant,

---

*The Rajput, or Rajhpoot, are nearly all of royal descent and are members of the highest military caste. Small men, they are fearless fighters. Their favorite weapon is a knife whose hilt is at right angles to the blade itself so that when they grip the hilt, the blade projects like an enlarged and sharp-edged knob on a set of "brass knucks". They strike with this knife like a pugilist delivering a jab—deadly and so fast it is almost impossible to parry since it carries all a man's striking weight behind it.

vicious action! With a twist and a roll, he had the knife and was springing to the attack! Only the fact that the Hindu was off-balance gave Wentworth a chance to avoid the first stroke of that deadly knife. With a quick backward spring, Wentworth flung the snake violently into the Hindu's face, but the man only brushed it aside and came swiftly on.

Wentworth held his gun, but he was loath to use it. If only he could force this man to talk! The Rajput glided forward like a boxer, left arm lifted as if it bore a shield, the right cocked with its broad blade jutting forward ahead of the knuckles. Used as a pugilist delivers a jab, it could strike a lightning-swift blow, almost impossible to parry. All the driving force of the man's weight would be behind it. Wentworth, dancing away, caught up a light chair and thrust the four legs toward the Hindu as a shield.

"I care not to kill you, Rajput," Wentworth said quietly, "but unless you drop that knife instantly, I'll shoot!"

For an instant, the Hindu appeared to hesitate, then the knife was flying straight at Wentworth's throat! It had been an incredibly fast throw, but Wentworth was ready. He jerked up the chair. The wide blade drove solidly into the seat, burst through and was checked only by the cross-grip that was its hilt. As quickly as he hurled the knife, the Rajput sprang for the door of the bathroom.

The *Spider's* gun pivoted easily—and still he held his fire. There was no exit to the bathroom save a small window that opened on eight stories of empty space. He still hoped to force the man to talk, and a shot would bring the entire hotel down about his ears, call in the police. Wentworth dropped the chair and angled toward the door. He moved warily. The man might carry another knife. The mirror door of the medicine cabinet gave him a partial view. A curse raked from Wentworth's lips. He caught a last glimpse of the man's legs vanishing through the small window!

Wentworth thrust himself backward from the door, ran reeling toward a window in the main room which opened beside that of the bathroom. He jerked up his gun to smash the glass, shook his head and strained at a stubborn sash. Finally, the window shrieked upward and he leaned out, gun ready. He had a glimpse of a dark body swinging against the side of the building, then a silvery glint of steel flashed at him. A strong contraction of his arm muscles thrust Wentworth inside just in time. He stumbled with the speed of his turn, reached the hall door in long bounds. He had seen enough. The Hindu's rope dangled from an open window two stories above his own. If he could reach the spot in time...

Imperceptibly, Wentworth's pace slackened, a smile twitched his lips and he came to a halt...beside the elevator doors. Within a minute and a half, he had engaged a taxi outside the building and had taken his stand at a corner which gave him a complete view of two sides of the building—the only sides on which there were exits. After the bravery the Rajput had displayed, it seemed extremely doubtful if even torture would force the man to talk. But he would have to report to his master the result of the attack. And when he did, Wentworth would be on his heels!

He smiled grimly.

IT WAS ten minutes before a small, furtive figure glided out of a service entrance and after walking three blocks entered a taxi. At Wentworth's signal, his own cab took up the trail. He glanced at his watch. Nine o' clock. Traffic would be heavy, and that would help them to keep the trail unobserved. But it would have to be quick. At ten o'clock, the Senate would convene for the day's work, which would include the bill to make Holme Secretary of Audit and Finance. Wentworth's lips shut grimly. If not the man himself, then men connected with him were criminals. He frowned, shook his head. What possible connection could there be between a United States Senator and a Rajput out of India? Wentworth realized that he could not be sure there was a connection! There might be absolutely no relation between the fact that Godlove had attempted to kidnap him, and, within ten minutes afterward, that Hindu had tried to murder him. There might be none, but—Wentworth's grim lips smiled sardonically—Elias Godlove would have to prove that to the Spider! Meantime, if this trail proved fruitful…

For half an hour, Wentworth followed the taxi which bore the Rajput through the tangle of early morning Washington traffic. Gradually, they pulled away from the more populous business streets and the stately homes of the residential area began to slip by. The cab ahead halted at the side entrance of a gracious red-brick mansion, whose white columns were vaguely familiar to Wentworth. He leaned forward sharply.

"Who's home is that?" he asked the driver.

The cab man grinned, "Senator from Indianois."

"Holme!" Wentworth cried.

"No, the other one. Senator Rufus Mayfrew!"

No one had descended from the other cab. Wentworth saw the driver jump to the pavement, jerk open the door of the back and lean inside. A moment later, he was staring wildly about, his arms waving excitedly.

"Stop by that cab!" Wentworth ordered shortly. He sprang down beside the other driver, strode past him to the door of the taxi. The Rajput was still inside, but it was almost impossible to recognize him. The face was swollen horribly, the flesh blue-black around two tiny torn punctures in the cheek. With a low oath, Wentworth realized what had happened. When he had thrown the *krait*, the teeth had accidentally struck there! He spun to the Hindu's driver.

"This is the address he gave you?" he demanded shortly.

The man nodded, swallowing hard. Wentworth strode swiftly to the front of the building and up the short walk between shrubbed lawns. His mind was racing furiously. He knew of Senator Mayfrew, of course. The man had been famous for years as a champion of the liberties of the people, for his opposition to vested interests. But Mayfrew had been equally bitter in recent months against his colleague from his own state, Senator Roger Holme. Holme had not been regularly elected, but appointed to fill the unexpired term of a senator who had died in office. The appointment, Wentworth had suspected at the time, had been more of a "kick upstairs" than a reward. An investigator of Holme's apparent acumen would be damned uncomfortable to a political machine.

So Indianois had preferred to have Holme do his work in Washington. And here Mayfrew had fought him—not the work he was doing, but the way in which he did it, his utter disregard of the liberties guaranteed by the Constitution. Yet the man who had attempted to kill Wentworth—whom Godlove apparently considered an enemy of Holme—had come directly to Mayfrew's home!

At the door, Wentworth presented his card, but was told that both Senator Mayfrew and Miss Ellen, his daughter who served him as secretary, had gone to the Capitol. The butler, an austerely proper Englishman, consented to view the body but could not identify the Rajput.

"No foreigners are employed in the master's retinue," he said coldly and marched back to his duties.

"You'd better call the police," Wentworth told the cab driver, sprang into his own taxi. "The Capitol," he ordered, "and make it fast."

The driver shook his head gloomily, "In this town, you can't," he said. "These confounded staggered lights are set for twenty-two miles and twenty-two is what you do, unless you got a siren like Senator Holme."

WENTWORTH chafed at the delay but forced himself to relax. He could not erase the frown from his forehead. The more deeply he probed this mystery the less clear it became. The ride was interminable. He took the steps of the Capitol at a walk so rapid it was almost a run. He would try the Senate cloakrooms first. Holme's card would get him past the doormen—but it didn't.

"Sorry, sir," the attendant said. "No visitors here now. There's a debate going on. You could go to the gallery."

"What debate?" Wentworth asked sharply.

The attendant stared at him curiously, "The one on a Secretary of Audit and..." He broke off. Wentworth was gone.

That appeal in the newspaper! How in the name of Heaven could he be expected to know what was threatening? But the reference had clearly been to this bill and, as Wentworth impatiently made his way to the galleries, he was conscious of a rising sense of danger. His eyes quested alertly about; there seemed no reason for alarm. The gallery was crowded despite the early hour. Abruptly, Wentworth's gaze focused and hardened. At the far end of the gallery, sat a man in a turban! Wentworth jerked his head angrily. Foolish to think, because a Hindu had attacked him, that all of that nationality were under suspicion! But the feeling of tension, of danger persisted.

Wentworth's eyes shifted to the floor of the Senate, itself. The voice of the speaker came to his ears distinctly. It was a voice that was strangely uncertain and hesitant.

"...And so I say to you, gentlemen, that if you vote this bill, you will destroy the personal liberties of the people. You allow a single man an authority which our forefathers fought a war to overthrow..."

"Mr. President!" Wentworth knew that bell voice, knew the tones of Senator Roger Holme. He pushed nearer to the gallery rail and stared below. Two men stood almost side by side down there, the challenging figure of Holme, the older, more dignified figure of another man with a silvery head. Wentworth recognized him also from many photographs. The original speaker then had been Senator Rufus Mayfrew!

"Mr. President!" Senator Holme intoned, "I wish to ask the permission of the other gentleman from Indianois to ask a question!"

Senator Mayfrew's figure seemed queerly shrunken. His shoulders were broad, but now they stooped. A great figure of a man who had been of pioneer stock, strong and sturdy and fearless. And yet...and yet now, as he gestured weakly in assent to the question Holme wished to ask, he seemed...*afraid!*

Senator Roger Holme, bowed gracefully, his bushy head of fiery hair momentarily lowered. "The question I wish to ask is this," he said, and his voice rang out in abrupt boldness. "Could it be possible that those who oppose my bill are afraid of it? Could it be possible that they fear what my investigations might reveal? What does my esteemed colleague think?"

Senator Holme sat down, and Rufus Mayfrew stood on his feet, a defeated man. His voice, when he spoke again, was almost inaudible. Abruptly, his head lifted.

"What do I think?" he cried. "I'll tell you what I think!" He stepped into the aisle and strode to the rostrum, not more than thirty feet from where Wentworth sat. "I think that if this bill is passed, the nation will be turned over to a crook and a thief, to a criminal who does not stop even at murder to attain his ends. That is my belief, gentlemen, and I back it with my life!"

THE SENATE chamber was in turmoil. Men were on their feet shouting to be heard. The gavel crashed and crashed again. But Wentworth was looking at none of these things. He was staring at Senator Mayfrew. He saw the man's hand go beneath his coat and he knew that gesture! Mayfrew held a gun. He...Wentworth shouted, but his cry was smothered in the uproar. Mayfrew had the gun in his hand now, but he was not pointing it at any one. He was staring down at it with a curious smile on his lips.

Wentworth's jaw snapped taut. No need for Mayfrew to announce his intention of suicide. Wentworth understood, as clearly as if the words had been shouted aloud, what had happened there on the floor. Senator Mayfrew, fighting the bill, had been threatened by Holme. He had defied Holme to deliver his blast and now he was taking the only way left to him, since he had made that defiance. He was going to kill himself. But he must not! It was apparent Mayfrew knew more about Holme and his conspiracy—Wentworth could not longer doubt that there was a criminal plot afoot!—and Mayfrew must be saved, at any cost.

Wentworth's thoughts were a flash through his brain. He put a hand on the gallery railing and climbed over, hung for a moment and dropped to the floor of the Senate. He fell clear in an aisle, but was unable to retain his balance. He staggered to his feet, heading for Mayfrew at a pelting run.

"No, Senator!" Wentworth shouted. "Mayfrew, for God's sake!"

Mayfrew's big head swung toward him. The gun was already presented at his own breast. He stared haggardly at Wentworth, sprinting toward him. Some obstruction caught Wentworth's ankle. He went down and before his eyes steel flashed, buried itself deeply in the floor—a knife! Some one had tried to kill him before he could reach Mayfrew! No time for that now. Wentworth was up and running.

"*Senator Mayfrew!*" he shouted.

Abruptly, the senator seemed to break loose from the lethargy which was upon him. He sprang toward where the Vice-President of the United States was pounding, pounding for order. In a half dozen great strides, he had reached the rostrum and sprung upon it. Mayfrew's great voice roared over the chamber.

"Gentlemen!" he cried. "Gentlemen, hear me a moment before—before I die!" Mayfrew stood there with the revolver presented to his temple, finger steady upon the trigger. The silence he commanded fell like darkness upon the chamber. Everywhere, men stopped in mad career, voices choked off in mid-word. All eyes were focused on Mayfrew, a proud and fighting silhouette high up on the rostrum.

"Gentlemen!" Mayfrew boomed. "I tell you this and then I die. If I have served my purpose, it is well. I have but one regret, that I have but one life to give for my country! Gentlemen, there is a conspiracy, a criminal conspiracy. Senator Holme—"

The shot that crashed out seemed to come from the senator's own gun. The force of lead hammered his head over on the left shoulder. His face contorted, his hands clenched and he drew up in a hideously contracted knot, arms and legs pulling toward his trunk for the half-second that he stood there upon the rostrum. Then stiffly, as a tree falls, he pitched to the floor, dead. Dead in the instant that lead had bored through his splendid brain, dead with words unspoken on his lips which must have shaken a nation to its foundations had they been uttered.

He fell at Wentworth's feet while he still fought to reach the man. Eagerly, Wentworth bent forward. If only he could catch one word, one word...But he knew it was futile. A man falls like that only when the blow has been instantly mortal. None could ever aid him now.

CHAPTER THREE
Sign Of The Cobra!

THE MOMENT of despair during which he bent over the dead senator seemed minutes long to Wentworth. Actually, only seconds elapsed. Then he was racing back across the bedlam of the Senate chamber. He passed a senator who stood stricken motionless, lips quivering like those of a terrified baby. Another had sprung upon his desk and was mouthing hoarse angry sounds, face mottled with fear. Everywhere, Wentworth saw the evidences of stark terror. His lips closed coldly on the curses that welled. Terror, yes—planned, deliberate terror! So that Roger Holme could impose his will upon a submissive Congress!

Wentworth skated to a halt beside the thing he sought, the knife hurled at him as he had raced to save Mayfrew. Its point was deep in the wood. Wrenching it free, Wentworth shot his keen gaze to the balconies. From the angle of the hilt, it had come from the far end there, and—A sharp exclamation burst from Wentworth's lips! The man with the turban! The Hindu had sat there and the thrown knife was a favorite weapon in his land.

A hand gripped Wentworth's shoulder and he twisted impatiently about, found himself looking into the grey face of a uniformed guard.

"You'll have to come with me, sir," he said harshly.

"Later, later!" Wentworth threw at him and streaked for the door. He ignored the guard's hoarse following shout, raced for the stairs that led to the gallery entrance. The long wide corridor echoed to the hammer of his feet. He palmed the marble balustrade, sprinted up the broad white steps. The upper corridor was filled with shouting, milling crowds, but Wentworth's eyes found at once the man he sought. Toward the Hindu, standing aloofly beside one of the high windows, Wentworth made his deliberate way, stood squarely before him. Wentworth bowed.

"I wish to return your knife!" he said crisply, presenting the weapon. "Your aim was bad. Very bad."

The Hindu met his gaze unfalteringly, almost mockingly, touched the knife hilt with his fingertips in refusal. Then his hand dropped carelessly to the green sash about his waist.

"The thanks of Rass Mehli for your intended kindness," he sail dryly. "I still have *my* knife." There could be no mistake about his mockery now, but Wentworth saw that he told the truth. There was a jewel-encrusted hilt at his waist. However, he had accomplished what he wished. The man would not have done anything so clumsy as to throw his only knife. Wentworth had merely intended to insist that he handle the weapon he had recovered, so as to get his fingerprints. This much the Hindu—had he called himself Rass Mehli?—had already performed for him.

Wentworth stepped back, satisfied now that there was some connection between this shrewd Oriental and the mystery that had brought him here. First, the Rajput assassin; now, a senator's suicide—and this mocking man in the gallery. What possible tie-up could there be? By the heavens, the *Spider* would pierce the mystery, and when he did…

As Wentworth straightened from his farewell bow, eyes once more on the Hindu's face, he barely suppressed a violent start. Was it possible that he had seen—what he believed he had? Rass Mehli also had bowed and when he bent his head a slanting ray of sunlight, curiously angling through a prismatic bevel of quartz window glass, had glanced across his forehead. For an instant, a painted symbol shone there, limned in brilliant red on the flesh where Brahmins were wont to wear the mark of their caste. It was gone almost at once, but Wentworth's shocked mind was convinced he had seen the symbol of—*the Cobra's Fangs!*

Some trick in the light rays had revealed it to him glancingly, and now it was gone. But in Heaven's name, why would this Hindu wear in Washington the secret insignia of an evil East Indian cult? Very little was known by white men of that occult Eastern order, but at mention of the *Cobra's Fangs* even Wentworth's brave Sikh, Ram Singh, grew enraged with the anger that fear breeds in the courageous. Against his will, Wentworth's eyes rested on the Hindu's forehead again, but there certainly was no symbol there now. Only the skin surface seemed a little duller than the surrounding flesh.

God! If that diabolic cult loosed its torture-worship on Washington, it meant greater horror than even the *Spider* had dreamed! But perhaps, the deviltry was already afoot! Perhaps, the reign of terror which had paralyzed the United States Senate and stricken one of its most noble figures was the work of the cult! With an effort almost physical, Wentworth pulled his eyes from the man's forehead.

There was a colder glitter in Rass Mehli's eyes. For a moment, the gaze of the two men locked. Very slightly, the Hindu smiled. His lips parted as if to speak—and a charge of angry men crushed Wentworth to the wall!

IT WAS as sudden as that. A brief rush of footsteps and Wentworth, turning to meet the attack, was borne backward, his shoulders nailed to the wall while striking fists and the gouging claws of men's hands reached viciously for him. It would have been easy for him to shoot a way out, but against his innocent fellowmen, the guns of the Spider were always holster-bound. With the skill of experience, he rolled the worst blows, crouched and used assailants' bodies as a shield, but he was badly mauled before a trumpeting voice stilled the onslaught, a voice he knew well and was beginning to hate!

"Don't kill him, men!" rolled the deep voice of Roger Holme. "There is a higher justice for the cowardly assassin of Senator Mayfrew!"

Wentworth heard the words, as he had the voice, with a sense of utter incredulity. Why, damn it, that little tin demi-god, Holme, was accusing him of murdering Mayfrew! Anger flared, but Wentworth fought it coldly down as—in the way it had once before—the crowd parted and permitted him to see face-to-face this man who grandiloquently styled himself the Sword of Justice! Fists still gripped Wentworth's arm and shoulders.

Holme's eyes were bitter, squeezed nearly shut by his angry frown. "You! *You!* And I saved your life at the airport last night—that you could murder the man I most love and revere!"

"Must you always make speeches!" Wentworth snapped at him. "If you used your eyes instead of your mouth, you'd know I was trying to save Mayfrew. It will be a matter of Congressional *Record* that you, Holme, threatened the senator just before he killed himself."

Holme shook his great head, made larger by the disorder of his thick, fiery, hair. His voice was as moving as organ music. "And to think," he whispered vibrantly, "that I offered

The shot that crashed out seemed to come from the senator's own gun.

you my friendship!"

Holme shuddered, turned half away as if he could not bear the thought. "Take him to face the girl he has orphaned!" he shouted then. "We'll see if he still can lie!"

Violently, despite his submission, Wentworth was harried through the long tumult-filled corridors while more furious men joined the mob with each second. Before him, with the bearing of a conquering Caesar bringing a rebel home in chains, marched Senator Roger Holme—and Wentworth was remembering that Holme had marched like this to demand the resignation of the mayor of Indianois City who had been burned alive by a mob!

Guards who should have turned them back from the tunnel to the Senate Office Building were sucked into the mob. Short of killing the men about him, Wentworth saw no escape. There might be greater opportunity in Mayfrew's offices. They were suddenly there and Wentworth was thrust through a doorway into the presence of a girl.

"Ellen!" Roger Holme cried. "I bring you the murderer of your father for justice!"

Wentworth gazed with frank admiration, despite the peril of his situation, at the tall girl who confronted him. She was statuesque, her hair of fiery gold bound like a coronet about her proudly held head. Although her face was drawn and pale, her blue eyes were clear and direct. This was Ellen Mayfrew, secretary and true daughter to him the people had called the Lion of the West. For a shocked instant her eyes widened on Wentworth, then a slight, wan smile touched her lips.

"Don't be silly, Roger," she said simply to Holme. "Dad committed suicide. He left me a note. And certainly this gentleman had nothing to do with it."

Holme's head jerked up in familiar challenge. "My eyes have seen!" he thundered.

Ellen Mayfrew looked at him and Wentworth watched curiously—quite as if his own life did not hang in the balance. He could feel the tense waiting of the mob behind him, and he knew their temper. He saw impatience in Ellen's face and a tenderness in her eyes that were like the eyes of a mother reproving her vaunting man-child. But her tone was sharp.

"If your eyes saw that," she said acidly, "You're cock-eyed. For Heaven's sake, Rog, be yourself. Don't make this horrible thing worse by a blunder of justice."

For an instant, a bewildered look crept over Holme's face as of a sleepwalker awakened. It vanished and he leveled a long, accusing arm at the girl.

"Unnatural daughter!" he cried. "Can it be that you are in league with your father's murderers!"

Ellen gasped, stiffened with rising anger. Wentworth felt his own wrath stir. Surely, the fool didn't intend to involve this lovely girl with the mob! Couldn't Holme see that Ellen—God help her!—loved him? Holme's voice ranted on. Wentworth's eyes flashed secretly about. Double peril hung over him now and over the girl. His lips tightened grimly. If he had to use his guns to save her, he would! The door behind him was packed with men. A half dozen had squeezed inside and their hands still gripped his arms and shoulders, but less fiercely. Yet there was no way out. The windows were high above the ground, and...

WENTWORTH was conscious of a strange murmuring in the crowd behind him, not of anger, but of some unidentifiable emotion. There was restless movement. He saw Ellen Mayfrew's face change, its lines stiffen into hostility, realized that Roger Holme had turned and stood with both hands held out eagerly. Abruptly, the savage grip on his shoulders was released and a softly warm hand touched Wentworth's own. He turned to meet darkly lustrous eyes, enormous in a face of utmost pallor—the same woman he had seen in Holme's car at the airport. She smiled at him before she turned to Holme.

"It has been revealed to me," she said in a rich deep voice, "that this man is innocent."

Wentworth's forehead contracted in a quick frown. What in the world did she mean, "revealed"? He was amazed at the change in Holme. His face was curiously radiant.

"You are sure, Yolanda?" he asked, barely above a whisper.

The woman called Yolanda stepped toward him. All her movements were slow and languorous like her voice, as stirring to a man's pulses as heady wine.

"When have I failed you?" she asked. "This man is innocent!" As she spoke, she turned once more to smile subtly upon Wentworth and he barely choked down a curse. In the center of her forehead, the skin was dull, as it had been on the brow of the Hindu, *exactly as if she, too, wore the sign of the Cobra's Fangs!*

It was at once apparent that her words were law to Senator Roger Holme. With the magic of his personality and voice, he dispersed what a few moments before had been a ravening mob. And the men cheered him hoarsely for his mercy as, a few moments before, they would have cheered his order to turn Wentworth alive! Wentworth's face was utterly impassive against the inner battering of his thoughts as Holme turned to him with a gallant bow.

"Forgive my error!" Holme said deeply, "and believe that it was only my deep grief and my rage at the assassin…"

"For Heaven's sake," Wentworth cut in sharply, "will you drop that mountebankery? I'm not one of your constituents. Talk like a human being instead of a windbag."

Abruptly, Holme flashed his boyish grin. "I said I liked you!" he cried. "Don't forget our date!"

WENTWORTH spun on his heel and stalked from the office. Ellen Mayfrew had dropped wearily into a seat, her proud head bowed for once. The woman, Yolanda, had not even glanced toward her, but stood in a curious immobility, her white hands clasped loosely before her, watching him from beneath the silken arches of her brows. Wentworth's bitter doubts hounded him furiously through the corridors toward the tunnel which connected with the Capitol. It would be a safer exit, even though the mob had dispersed. He had no wish to injure anyone, if they should decide to attack again.

His brain was tormented. A diabolic Indies cult which could claim a lovely woman like Yolanda and that subtle Hindu, Rass Mehli, as fellow conspirators, apparently could dictate to the powerful Roger Holme. And yet there was no dull spot on his forehead to mark him as one of the Cobra's men. But that only deepened the mystery, the thickening, menacing cloud that clung over the capital city. Ellen Mayfrew's certainty of her father's suicide was strange.

Wentworth stopped short. By Heaven, it was ridiculously obvious. It must have been Mayfrew who had uttered that frantic appeal to the *Spider!* Then the *Spider* must pay a call to Mayfrew's daughter!

Meantime, he must track to its lair the members of the vile cult of the Cobra. Wentworth realized he had reached the entrance of the tunnel to the Capitol. The entrance was unguarded. The discipline of the personnel had been completely disrupted by the tragedy in the Senate Chamber. Wentworth whipped open the door and strode through—came up on his toes in a split-second halt. One of the automobiles which shuttled through the tunnel for the senators' convenience was parked opposite him. From the tonneau, a man pointed a machine gun directly at him!

As his quick eyes spotted the assassin, two other men moved tensely around the ends of the car, guns ready in their fists. All three men were Hindus, though they wore no turbans, Wentworth realized, and on the forehead of each glimmered—the ominous sign of the Cobra!

With a furtive hand, Wentworth tried the door behind him. It would not budge, immovably locked from the other side in the brief second since his entrance. It was a neat trap, neatly sprung…God alone knew how he could escape! His sharp glance swept the entire scene. No slightest particle of cover and no retreat. The two men with automatics came to a halt. They had him bracketed for perfect cross-fire. The teeth of the man in the car

Richard Wentworth

showed whitely in a smile. He lined the machine gun's sights on Wentworth's body. The *Spider's* lips drew tight and still. His hands dangled emptily at his sides. Swiftly as he could draw his twin guns, he knew that before he could go into action, a dozen bullets would rip through his body!

"Very well," he said quietly, "I surrender."

The machine gunners smile widened, "There is no question of surrender, Wentworth *sahib*," he said strongly. "It is merely that you must die!"

CHAPTER FOUR
Storm Troops Of Death

FIGHTING MEN have said that no one can spring into violent action without telegraphing advance warning of his intention to his opponent by some sign, a change of expression, a flicker of watchful eyes, the tensing of muscles. Perhaps these men had never known such a one as the Spider in whom keen brain and finely muscled body were refined by training to the ultimate perfection of coordination. It is a fact that before the Hindu had ceased speaking, Wentworth made his gamble for life.

Without even a preliminary tautening of muscles, he hurled himself violently to the left and toward one of the automatic-armed Hindus! The machine gun bellowed and only hemstitched the doors against which Wentworth had stood. Elation bounded high in his heart. His whole desperate plan depended on making the machine gunner miss his first burst. And in that he had succeeded. Laughter burst from his lips, the flat, mocking laughter of the *Spider!*

Wentworth knew that though many Hindus were excellent rifle shots, their hands turned more readily to knives for close action. He gambled on their inexpertness with their present arms. If the machine gunner knew his business, he would cut that first burst off instantly because otherwise the savage recoil of the speedy Thompson gun he held would make it impossible to swing the weapon around swiftly. He hoped that the Hindus with the automatics would either depend on the machine gunner doing his job, or become flustered and inaccurate during action. A terrific gamble with more than life at stake—with a nation's life at stake!

The machine gunner held his trigger an instant too long while he fought to swing the weapon around. Even as he leaped, Wentworth's gun-swift hands flashed to the automatics beneath his arms. As his feet struck earth again, he checked sharply for the infinitesimal fraction of time necessary to make sure of his first shots. If they failed, there would be no time for a second! He could not even wait to see the effect of his fast-flung lead, but pivoted and hurled headlong for the nearest Hindu, now no more than fifteen feet away.

The man's lips were snarled back from his teeth. He was leaning forward on slim legs and he threw out a shot as a man would throw a knife. The gun leaped in his hand and powder-flame lanced toward Wentworth. Almost, he felt its fiery tongue lick his face, but it was somewhere else the bullet had struck. Wentworth's breath drove out of his lungs. The middle of his body went numb. His two guns blasted together. Ahead of him, the Hindu was blown backward, literally snapped off his feet and slammed against the back of the car by the combined impact of two .45 caliber bullets.

The force of Wentworth's own leap was checked. His feet struck, but could not feel the ground. Failing, he managed to twist his body, and pitched backward with his guns lined along the side of the car, toward the third

Hindu at its front. Wentworth fired and something slammed down heavily across his chest—the body of the Hindu he had slain. Dimly, he realized that the machine gunner must be dead, too. That chattering weapon could not otherwise have been silent so long. But there was still a man on his feet throwing lead and Wentworth could not see him. Deliberately, with leaden slowness it seemed to Wentworth, he released his left gun and gripped the body that lay across him. He heaved, and then he could see.

The third Hindu was surging toward him with great leaps, gun hurled aside. In his right hand, he gripped a knife along whose blade the light ran coldly. Even as Wentworth spotted him, his hand whipped back for a throw. Twice, and a third time Wentworth dragged on the trigger of his automatic. There could be no aiming. His first bullet caught the Hindu in a lifted leg, flung the limb backward and to the side as if it were a pendulum struck by a sledge-hammer. The impact whirled the assassin half-about. His knife flew high and its thin tinkle against the wall came somewhere between Wentworth's second and third shots, and blended with the scream that poured terribly from the man's mouth. That sound finished, too, cut short with the curt blast of the third shot, and it was a dead man which hit the pavement. His head bounced and nudged gently against Wentworth's right shoe.

METHODICALLY, Wentworth began to tug his way clear of the body which lay upon him. Blood was smeared across his own chest, but whether his own or the Hindu's he did not know. There was a hoarse, whistling sound which pierced even his blast-deadened eardrums and he knew, with a start, that it was his breathing. He got free of the body and sat up. Pain was beginning to touch him now, but it was not the sharp agony of an air-filled wound. It was dull. More like a—punch. Wentworth's groping hands came away from his abdomen with a battered piece of metal. His belt buckle. The flesh was torn, but the bullet's blow must have been glancing. Wentworth laughed shakily and pushed to his feet. His lips shut off the sound grimly. By the heavens, this time the Cobra should have an answer!

Wentworth bent sharply above the two slain men at his feet and the opened base of his cigarette-lighter now ground against the dead flesh where the sign of the Cobra glimmered. When he straightened, that diabolical insignia was blotted out by another which to the guilty brought dread and cold terror, by a vermilion seal with hairy legs and poisonous fangs—*the seal of the Spider!*

Wentworth peered into the car, grimly. It was plain that both of his bullets had struck the machine gunner. One bullet couldn't do that much damage to a man's head! Sound was running along the tunnel now, the raucous note of men's excited voices, the heavy beat of their feet. With long strides that still faltered a little, Wentworth reached the door through which he had entered. It was no longer locked. The bullets of the machine gun had smashed the fastening to bits. Wentworth's lips twitched a little. That lock had been just behind his back…

It was five minutes later, when a car was bearing Wentworth swiftly back toward his hotel, that he jerked erect with a sharp realization of what he had done. Men sent to murder Wentworth had been slain—by the *Spider!* It would be sufficient evidence for his enemies. He had betrayed himself. He would have to leave the hotel at once, go into hiding. But he knew where to strike, where to seek his enemies. If he had needed confirmation of his suspicion concerning that dull spot upon the forehead of the woman called Yolanda, he had it in plenteous measure! It had been Yolanda who had freed him from the clutches of the mob and sent him to die at the hands of the Cobra killers! Doubtless, this had been done so that Holme, himself, would bear no taint of blame…

IT TOOK Wentworth seven minutes to throw his things together and leave the hotel. He rented a powerfully motored sedan and, with his suitcases in it, parked in a deserted, tree-lined street. With shades drawn, he went swiftly to work before a small mirror, though the thing that he did was so familiar to his hands they might have performed it perfectly in the dark. A lotion sallowed his cheeks and drew the skin tautly across the bones. Make-up putty changed his nose into a predatory beak beside which his eyes seemed small and sinister. The chiseling of his lips was painted out so that his mouth became a straight gasp in a hard-boned face. That was all, except for bushy black brows over his own, a lanky black wig and—it was the face of the Spider!

Wentworth studied the face intently before he nodded. But he was not yet through. He brushed the eyebrows out smoothly, added a Van Dyk beard with waxed mustaches. Swiftly, then, he changed to dark clothing, a broad brimmed black hat. In precisely a half hour after he left, he parked the car beside the Senate Office Building, where police officials still milled about the scene which the *Spider's* guns and the *Spider's* seal had marked. Wentworth avoided them and made his way directly to the office of the late Senator Mayfrew. There he had last seen Yolanda, and there he would pick up the trail that led to the den of the Cobra. Wentworth's doubts were gone. Whatever the secret of the alliance, he could no longer doubt that Senator Roger Holme and the Cobra's Fangs were partners in a fearful conspiracy of murder and loot!

A frown made a vertical crease between Wentworth's eyes as he approached Mayfrew's office from which the last of a group of obvious newspaper men was issuing. Ellen Mayfrew had mentioned a note left by her father. If he could see that, it might offer some clue to the senator's reasons for suicide. To Wentworth, the suicide seemed plainly intended to block passage of the Holme bill, and Mayfrew headed the opposition to Holme...

The devil! Why hadn't he guessed before that Mayfrew might have inserted the advertised appeal to the *Spider!* He was the logical man. Excitement raced in his veins as Wentworth bowed to Ellen Mayfrew from the doorway.

"My condolences on your loss," he said thickly, assuming an accent. "I know of no *Cicero* we could less afford to lose."

Ellen's eyes widened. She pushed up from her seat with stiffened arms braced on the desk. "Won't you come into the inner office," she asked breathlessly. Impulsively, her hands went out to Wentworth. "Oh, if only you had arrived a few hours earlier!" she whispered. "Father knew so much more and I know so little! You..." She bit her lips. "But I...do not know you! Who are you that you use that...word?"

Wentworth smiled slightly and his cupped hand rested for an instant upon a sheet of stationery. When it was lifted, the vermilion seal of the *Spider* glowed there! Only for a moment did Wentworth permit it to be seen, then he had touched fire to the paper.

"Let me urge you," he told Ellen quietly, "to talk swiftly and tell me all you know—and about Holme and this succubus, Yolanda. And why Hindus of the Cobra's Fangs should support Holme!"

Ellen Mayfrew sagged into a chair, covered her eyes with a hand. "In just a moment," she said weakly. "I have been waiting so long...Yolanda Blanton—she is a widow still under thirty—has an eleven-year-old son, lives on Sixteenth Street, Northwest. I can find you the address. I don't know how Roger Holme met her but...You called her a succubus, I think? She is that all right. She feeds on his soul! She is the one who will destroy him, inflating his ego until he believes himself little less than a god. I...I think she's his...mistress and has been since before they left Indianois."

WHILE her words poured out, Wentworth's eyes and ears kept watch. He had sensed terror behind her demand for proof of his identity—and justified terror, he suddenly knew! Had it not driven one of the nation's leading men to suicide? Where that could happen, other men must be swayed by that same fear, their votes subject to orders from criminals!

At a brisk question, Ellen laughed a little. "Roger head of the conspiracy? Oh, he's such a kid, *Spider!*" she cried. "He's not capable of it. It's that woman, Yolanda Blanton!"

Slowly, Wentworth shook his head. "Think again," he urged. "She's only a tool. Some man's tool." He made swift mental note of the men she mentioned, Daniel Borough, publisher of the newspaper through which Holme had issued the first revelations of graft which made him mayor in his home city. Borough was with him constantly. Bruce Calvin, Jr., was the angel of the Populist Party, whose standard Holme carried. He had thrown tens of thousands into the war chest.

"Dad and I found that out through a friend in the income-tax division," she said. "Then there's the Swami Re, a fortune teller that many people go to here in Washington. He calls himself a yogi. Does that sound foolish?"

Wentworth said softly, "Many things sound mad. Yet Hindus tried to kill me twice today—and your father committed suicide."

Much of Ellen's bravery seemed to have left her now. It was as if she had borne up strongly for this interview and when it was accomplished, strength went out of her. Her voice was faint as she said, "I never liked that Elias Godlove."

Wentworth rose abruptly, "And your father left me no message?"

"I know so little," Ellen insisted. "I only know that he was terribly alarmed—and frightened. He told me his 'honor pulled him both ways.' But he wouldn't explain what he meant. He had counted on talking to you before the bill came up, but it was called to vote early. And Dad accomplished nothing by dying—not even a delay. They're voting on it now!"

Wentworth cried out sharply—voting already on the bill to create the post of Secretary of Audit and Finance! It seemed incredible that on a day of tragedy, the Senate would continue in session.

"Roger is responsible for that," Ellen went on dully. "He made a speech and said that Dad—that it was proof that investigation was needed! Oh, sometimes I think Roger is mad!"

Wentworth's brain was racing but nothing short of murder would prevent...A buzzer sounded faintly, then a clerk's dry voice came over the annunciator.

"The United States has just voted, sixty-four to thirty-one..."

Ellen cried out, "That's enough to pass over a veto!"

"...for the bill numbered 2764 and entitled 'A Bill to make compulsory a new cabinet position of Secretary of Audit and Finance and to provide for the appointment within twenty four hours of said secretary."

Ellen's eyes filled. "Poor Dad," she whispered. "You know, *Spider*, that bill provides that if the Senate three times disapproves the President's nominee, it can appoint one of its own members arbitrarily."

The clerk's voice was rasping on. "Attached to the bill is a resolution memorializing the President of the United States to appoint at once the surviving gentleman from Indianois, the Honorable Roger Holme."

With a low oath, Wentworth strode sharply from the office. It would do no good to kill Holme if he were a figurehead only. In any case, in this enormous conspiracy, his death would bring only a temporary check. His "martyrdom"—they would call it that!—would give the conspiracy a weapon to smash all opposition. They could proscribe all powerful enemies for the assassination.

No, no murder, Holme must live to expose the conspiracy and its allies to vengeance...Daniel Borough. First of all, Wentworth must locate and investigate the publisher who had given Holme his start. Ellen had said he was rarely far from Holme's side. He would be easy to identify, a broad-beamed man who clung to quasi-western garb.

AHEAD OF Wentworth, the doors of the Senate chamber flung wide and cheering men streamed out behind the conquering hero. Wentworth was beginning to hate the challenging posture of Roger Holme, the brazen egotism of his stride. Beside him padded a bluffly red-faced man in a long frock coat whom

Wentworth identified at once as the publisher, Borough. His face was one broad smile. Everywhere, that smiling joy. Damn the fools, didn't they realize what threatened?

From across the corridor Elias Godlove, striding leanly, advanced to meet his master and Wentworth stared at the man in amazement. Godlove wore a uniform such as Wentworth had never seen before! Modeled exactly on the uniform of an American army officer, it was of rich dark green and flittered with golden emblems! In Heaven's name, what did it portend! Wentworth knew—but scarcely dared to give the thought a name. Godlove was ushering Roger Holme out to the broad steps of the Capitol with such homage as a subject might render a revered king. As they moved along the broad corridor, other men in the strange green uniform fell in and marched in swinging ranks like a guard of honor!

Wentworth had overtaken the group of worshipping senators now and was thrusting through their straggling ranks. Violently, he slammed out to the portico of the Capitol—and halted, rigid with anger and dread of the thing he saw. In solid ranks, more than a thousand green-uniformed men jammed the plaza. At sight of Holme, their arms were flung high in a dramatic salute and with the gesture their voices lifted in a swelling deep roar:
"Hail, Chief! Hail! Hail!"

Afterward, a complete silence fell and Godlove's nasal voice rose strongly.

"Hail, Chief!" he repeated, standing at salute. "We are your men! We are your storm troops for righteousness and justice! The Holme Guard! One million strong, we salute you from every State of the Union with these words: 'Hail Chief! Hail! Hail!'"

And with his last words, the deep-toned salute rolled from the ranks of the Holme Guard again, ominous as crashing thunder on a night of awful calm.

That was the frightful spectacle which Richard Wentworth gazed upon.

CHAPTER FIVE
Assassination!

AS THE significance of the thing that was happening here beat in upon Wentworth's consciousness, his hands lifted instinctively toward his guns. Before his very eyes, the action that people said could not happen here was taking place. A dictator had been born—a dictator allied with criminals and a diabolical cult out of the East. Wentworth forced his hands from his guns. Death would not help. He flung a frantic, questioning glance about.

The publisher toward whom Ellen Mayfrew pointed as a possible conspirator, Daniel Borough, stood just behind Holme, and there was no one else near save Godlove and the guard of honor. Most of the senators had stopped inside the Capitol, but one man stood quietly to one side of the doors and Wentworth remembered sharply that he had seen the man stand so earlier when Mayfrew's suicide had thrown the Senate chamber into an uproar. The face was familiar…By heavens, it was Senator Martin Ipswich, who no later than the previous session had made a name for himself as an investigator. Could he be involved in any way?

The shot came as an exclamation point to Wentworth's fears. It came from before the Capitol steps and became a burst of rapid firing. Wentworth whirled, but resisted the impulse to draw his gun. Instantly, he spotted the source of the shots. One of the uniformed Holme Guards had leaped from the ranks. His gun was held deliberately before him, as steadily as on target range. He was firing…at Senator Roger Holme! But Holme was untouched. That was immediately apparent. His head thrown back, he stepped strongly forward—and laughed! His booming laughter swept out over the heads of the Holme Guard.

"This was foretold!" Holme cried. "But you cannot harm me. No bullet can change my destiny."

It was only then Wentworth saw that another man had not been so fortunate. The bluff Daniel Borough had taken at least two of the bullets in his body for his shirt was stained red. As the last shot ripped out, he slumped to his knees and swayed there an instant before he pitched forward and rolled over limply an his back.

These things happened in fractions of a second. As Borough fell, the storm trooper hurled his gun wildly at Holme, turned and ran. Scarcely a moment later, Wentworth leaped down the steps and streaked after him. If he could overtake the man and help him to escape, he might learn the answers to many questions. Obviously, this man hated Holme.

Wentworth was fully aware of the risk he ran. These fanatic storm troopers would swarm after the fleeing assassin. And Wentworth, running, immediately involved himself as accomplice…Wentworth groaned aloud as he saw the green-clad ranks splitting to bits, dozens of men whirling in their tracks to race after the killer. He would be too late! But the man was running wonderfully, head thrown back, legs pistoning like a champion.

Whether they caught the man or not, Wentworth knew, this attempt spelt horror. As he had foreseen when he, himself, had considered the necessity of Holme's death, there would be wholesale reprisals that would strengthen Holme's position. Wentworth changed his direction, sprinted across the angle of the man's flight. He could make sure with a few shots that the man would escape. Only a few of his pursuers threatened to overtake him, but he could not fire. The guards were guilty of no crime save hero-worship. That it might grow into a menace which would sweep America's democracy from the face of the earth meant nothing…

This thing must stop.

IT WAS when Wentworth was almost certain that the assassin, streaking through the parked trees of the Capitol lawn, would escape that the blow fell. Squarely into the man's path two persons, a woman and a man in the gray uniform of a Capitol guard. With a gasped curse, Wentworth recognized the woman. She was…Yolanda! A gun glinted in the guard's hand, spoke once sharply. The fugitive's leg whipped out from under him and he sprawled headlong to the ground. Even then, he fought to get to his feet and escape, but it was too late. A half-dozen men in green hurled themselves upon him and scores, hundreds of others raced to the attack.

Yolanda's voice rose tremendously, piercing through the roaring anger of the men.

"His accomplice!" she shouted. "Pull down his accomplice!"

She was pointing directly at Wentworth! Instantly, a dozen faces jerked toward him and men began to close in at a run.

"Lynch them!" cried Yolanda! "Burn them alive! They tried to kill our chief!"

A hysterical shout of approval roared up from the men. The Capitol guard apparently the only one who carried a gun, was angling for a clear shot. Across the heads of other racing harriers, Wentworth glimpsed his face and it was white and set. Vaguely, he recognized the man as the same who had attempted to detain him after Mayfrew's suicide.

The Holme men were dragging the assassin along the ground by his wounded leg. He cried out in agony and his voice reached Wentworth thinly. "Traitors!" he was shouting at them. "You tricked me, damn you! I was supposed…"

A storm trooper deliberately kicked him in the mouth. His words strangled and became unintelligible. And suddenly Wentworth grasped the truth. The assassination—hadn't Holme shouted it was foretold?—had been planned to give an excuse for proscribing enemies. This poor devil, picked for the job, would be sacrificed. With a thin smile on his lips, Wentworth whipped out his gun.

"Stand back!" his voice, no more than a whisper, cut savagely across the interval that separated him from the men closing in upon him. "Stand back—or you die!"

A few wavered, but more pushed steadily forward, and behind them Yolanda's voice ran on and on, tolling them madly to the kill. Wentworth threw a bullet over the heads of the men, started forward at a dead run. Perhaps he still had a chance to rescue that assassin. The man deserved death, but not yet—not while, angrily, he might pour information into the *Spider's* ears.

One of the troopers caught up a stone and hurled it viciously at Wentworth's head. He dodged easily, ran straight at the man. He heard shouts behind him, a wild chorus of yells and realized that he had sprung into action just in time. He was surrounded, and in a few moments more would have been pulled down from behind!

As Wentworth charged, the man leaped forward to meet him. A dodge, a quick flicking blow with one of his guns, and the man spilled hard to the earth. Wentworth went racing on. Guns were beginning speak. The Capitol guard was on one knee, revolver braced against a tree trunk. From behind, lead whistled on a high, savage note. Wentworth pulled his head down, zigzagged like a football runner in a broken field.

He was barely fifty feet from the captive assassin when one of the guards spotted him. Instantly, a gun was in the man's hand. He fired, point-blank—into the assassin's skull! Only afterward did he fling himself prone and open fire on Wentworth.

The very unexpectedness of the man's action in killing the prisoner almost proved fatal to Wentworth. He faltered in his stride, and the man's first shot caught him flat-footed. The bullet whimpered by so close his cheek felt the hot breath of its passage. Deliberately, Wentworth stumbled and cried out hoarsely. The next bullet flew wide, and Wentworth leaped high in his running, plunged to the ground in a roll that sent him crashing into a clump of shrubbery.

IT WOULD be simple to escape now; a dodging, crouched run through the bushes could carry him swiftly away from danger. Instead, Wentworth hid motionless in the shrubbery and with deft fingers removed the false beard and mustache he wore. If he had had any doubts of the accuracy of his guess that the assassination was part of a deliberate plan of the conspirators, that death-shot had removed them. It became even more imperative that he capture a man who could be forced to reveal the further details of the plot.

Alertly, Wentworth spied through the tangle of branches and leaves. His virtual vanishment had thrown many of the troopers off his trail. The shooting had disconcerted others, for it was apparent most of the Holme Guard were unarmed. They turned from the chase to converge on the assassin's body, still being dragged back toward the Capitol. They pelted the corpse with stones and branches torn from trees; they kicked and jumped upon it in a frenzy of rage. But the gunman who had opened fire darted toward Wentworth's cover and two other men flanked him, automatics in hand.

Without a betraying sound or movement of bushes, Wentworth wriggled his way upgrade to a position twenty feet to one side of the place he had fallen. While he crawled, he searched the ground. There were few rocks— only one of the size he needed. He picked up that and a handful of dusty clods of earth. With this pile of feeble ammunition before him, he waited—waited until the first man was only twenty feet from the shrubs and the others slightly behind and to the sides.

"That's where the guy fell," the leader said. "You can see where he hit the ground."

They were right about that. What they did not know was that Wentworth now was twenty feet to their left. Wentworth caught up his one rock, weighted it carefully on his palm—he did not wish to kill—and hurled it at the head of the rearmost man! His aim was good. The rock caught the man just above the ear and dropped him, unconscious, to the ground. At the sound of the fall, the other two men spun about, guns questing, but there was nothing to indicate how the man had been felled or from what direction the blow had come. One fired wildly at a movement in the shrubs and a bird popped out, twittering. That was all.

The leader swore hoarsely, sprang into the bush and thrashed about with his gun. Wentworth caught up his clods of dirt, tucked his guns into his belt. He was near the outer fringe of the shrubs, his pursuers deep in the thicket. Softly, Wentworth sent the mocking, flat laughter of the *Spider* toward the men.

They whirled, cursing, and Wentworth swiftly threw two handfuls of dusty clods. The guns of the men crashed, but without direction, then the clods burst against their faces, filled their eyes and nostrils with stinging dust. While they still pawed at their faces, Wentworth darted forward on swift, silent feet. His heavy guns swung carefully—and two more of the Holme Guard lay unconscious on the ground.

It was the work of minutes to strip one of the men and don his uniform, to shoulder the leader's unconscious body and jog toward the Capitol. Presently, he began to pass stragglers of the guard.

"Wounded," he gasped. "Got to get him to the hospital. Clear the way."

Men took up his shout, ran before him. In a few minutes, Wentworth broke clear of the trees, lined toward his parked car and, seconds later, had tossed the limp body into the back of his sedan and was roaring through the Capitol drives. But there was no smile of triumph on the *Spider's* lips. Too much peril threatened the city and the nation, the valiant leaders of the country. When the Holme Guard began its reprisals, undoubtedly carefully planned by the evil genius behind their actions, the United States would be shaken to its very foundations!

Soon Wentworth slowed his headlong flight, took time to bind and gag his prisoner. For the first time, he had a clear view of the man's face and Wentworth swore softly. The man was a gang killer from New York, a murderer notorious for his cruelty, his utter ruthlessness with his victims. Truly, Senator Holme picked curious recruits for his Storm Troops of Justice! Well, his choice made the *Spider's* task easier. He need have no compunctions about the methods he used to make Gat Warton talk!

WENTWORTH'S phone call caught Ram Singh within an hour of his Sikh servant's arrival at the Hoover Airport and forty-five minutes later they had the gun killer, Gat Warton, at a lonely spot in the near-by Virginia Hills. They made sure Warton was conscious before they began preparations by stripping him to the waist and spread-eagling him on his back, legs and arms tied to four saplings.

Gat Warton began to whine almost at once, but Wentworth and his bearded Sikh ignored that. They laid wads of cotton, soaked in alcohol in a curious design on his chest—the symbol of the *Spider*. Then Ram Singh, struck a match…

"Hey, for God's sake!" Warton cried. "Lay off. You…you wouldn't strike a match to that, would you? Hell, it would burn clean through to my lungs!"

Ram Singh bent imperturbably forward with the match. "Not quite," he said casually. "No, I have never seen it quite reach the lungs."

Gat Warton shrieked and strained at his bonds. Wentworth said quietly, "Just a minute."

"Do not stop me, master!" Ram Singh pleaded. "Let me give him at least a little sample, lest the fool think we are men to trifle with!"

Wentworth appeared to consider, shrugged and nodded—and Ram Singh struck another match

"For God's sake, master!" Gat Warton shrieked. "Call off the smoke. I don't need no sample. If you want to know anything, I'll talk! I'll squeal all over the place!"

Warton began to babble. He was in the Holme Guard along with half a hundred of his kind because word had gone around in New York that high wages awaited big shots in various criminal lines if they would sign up with the guard in Washington.

"Hell!" Warton crowed. "They pay me two-fifty a week with a bonus of a grand every time I bump somebody they think needs it."

"Was that the price for murdering that Holme Guard who killed Borough?" Wentworth asked quietly.

Gat Warton nodded eagerly. "Hell, imagine that guy bumping a swell egg like Borough!" he croaked. "It was a pleasure to shoot him."

Wentworth smiled slightly. "Start the fire," he directed Ram Singh quietly.

Warton squealed. "I'm talking! I'm talking!" he cried. "Geez, what do you want?"

"The truth!" Wentworth told him coldly. "Perhaps, my friend, you did not notice the design in which that fire is laid, the design it will presently burn down to your lungs if I am not satisfied with your answers. Look at it again, Warton."

Fearfully, Warton pulled up his head and stared down at the cotton tracery on his chest. His face went dead white and he sagged limply in his bonds.

"God," he whispered. "The *Spider!* Listen, I'll spill. This mug was primed to bump Borough off. This dame they call Yolanda goes into a trance and says Borough is two-timing Holme and this mug volunteers to bump him. So I get my orders that, after it's done, I'm to bump the mug, see?"

"You got your orders how?" Wentworth demanded.

Warton shivered in the confines of his bonds. "It was screwy," he said, "and it scared me silly. One of the other guards—guy I never saw before—tells me he's got orders for me and I goes with him to some smelly dump and we goes down in the basement. And all at once, I'm in some sort of church or something and there's a idol up there with six arms waving in the air..."

Ram Singh drew in a hissing breath and Wentworth's eyes tightened. No doubt about what idol the man meant. Siva, the Terrible. Siva of the Seven Destroying Arms! Evil god of the cult of the Cobra's Fangs!

"Where?" Wentworth demanded. "Where was this temple you were taken to?" He bent forward sharply.

Gat Warton opened his mouth to speak, but no words issued from his throat. As Wentworth bent forward, he heard the hiss of a swift missile pass him by, felt the chill of its close passage by his throat. And a knife pierced, up to its hilt, in the heart of Gat Warton!

CHAPTER SIX
Siva The Terrible!

WENTWORTH, already bending forward, dropped flat on his face across the body of Gat Warton, rolled sharply to his left and whipped an automatic from its under-arm holster. Instantly, it was bucking in his hand, hurling lead into the blackness behind him. Wentworth had no target but his split-second reflexes already had estimated the course of that thrown knife and his bullets truly retraced its path.

Ram Singh had sprung backward from beside Warton and his throwing knife cut a silver gash in the early darkness. Wentworth's roll carried him to his feet and he darted to the attack, Ram Singh running lightly beside him. Ahead of them a man groaned hoarsely and there was a single crash in the shrubbery. Abruptly, Wentworth halted. His outflung arm stopped the faithful Sikh. At their feet lay a turbaned Hindu. There were two bullets in his chest. One had fractured the right collar bone, the other had drilled the heart. The hilt of Ram Singh's knife jutted from the man's throat. And on his forehead glimmered the hateful sign of the Cobra!

"To the road!" Wentworth whispered. "Silently!"

They separated and were swallowed into the dusk beneath the trees. Moments later, both emerged on the lonely lane which branched from the main road a mile away. Behind their own car a coupe was parked. It was empty and, though they waited for minutes, they heard and saw nothing further.

"He was alone," Wentworth concluded, and he cursed bitterly. He had learned from Gat Warton no more than a confirmation of his own fears and a hint of other, more perilous things before that knife had cut short his confessions. And he had been forced to kill the knife-thrower lest death for him and Ram Singh flash also from the darkness. But he had learned one useful thing—the order for Borough's death had come through Yolanda Blanton.

A deep frown cut his forehead at that thought. Yolanda also had brought a message which she called a "revelation" to Holme. What was all this talk of revelations and foretelling? This trance in which Yolanda had revealed Borough's supposed traitorousness? Wentworth's memory flashed back to his talk with Ellen Mayfrew. She had mentioned a Swami Re, who played the role of occult yogi in the capital. Occultism and Hindu knife killers; a Congress that jumped at a whisper from Holme...

"Back to the city!" Wentworth ordered crisply. "We will let the dead dogs lie!"

He hurried back into the darkness of the woods and stopped a moment beside each of the bodies. On the forehead of each, he pressed the base of his cigarette-lighter and imprinted the seal of the *Spider!* Let it strike terror to the hearts of the criminals the conspirators were calling to their aid! Trained gunmen in the ranks of the Holme Guard which Godlove had called Storm Troops of Justice! And that was not the end—Warton had said before he died that big shots in all lines had been brought to Washington, a Congress of Crooks in the nation's capital! Here was a nightmare!

Swiftly, he hurled the sedan back along the Virginia roads toward Washington, throwing crisp orders at Ram Singh. "I have made out a list of the chief enemies of Senator Holme," he instructed. "Undoubtedly, they will be the first that are struck in the reprisals. You will phone or visit each of them and say this:

" 'Holme's guards are coming to seize you. They will charge you with the murder by conspiracy of Daniel Borough, and say it was an attempt to murder Holme. You have only one chance and that is to flee. Heed this warning if you wish to live, and defeat this conspiracy to seize the government. The *Spider* gives you this warning'."

Flight by these men meant surrender to the menace of Holme, but better that than death! When the conspiracy had been smashed, they would be alive to overthrow by legislative action whatever criminal laws Holme set up. Dead, they would be replaced—and Wentworth could not doubt that Holme, or the conspirators behind him, had arranged for their successors to be Holme men.

"Where do you go, *sahib?*" Ram Singh asked as they sped back across the broad Potomac.

Wentworth gave him the address. "The woman, Yolanda Blanton, is a mouthpiece for the chief criminal. It is through her they give orders. I must find a way to force the truth from her!"

RAM SINGH dropped from the car and Wentworth skimmed through park drives, across Pennsylvania Avenue and into the broad stretch of Sixteenth Street. The address Ellen Mayfrew had given him for Yolanda, proved to be a large private mansion, set among formally planted lawns. Wentworth circled the block and, parking, approached it from the rear. He was frowning. The task that lay ahead of him was not to his liking, but it was increasingly apparent that she was the key to the situation. The Spider could not shirk.

It was completely dark, a moonless night and Wentworth slid, as silently as the creature whose name he bore, through the shadows to the back lawn, crept toward Yolanda's mansion. Patiently, he searched for guards, but despite a half hour's careful scrutiny of the place, succeeded in locating none. Grimly then, Wentworth prepared to invade the house itself. He would have to take his chances with these hidden guards.

A thick-leafed tree bowed near the rear portico and Wentworth—clad now in the low-crowned black hat, the black cape the world knew as the habiliments of the *Spider*—climbed swiftly up this tree. Only the faint creak of a limb betrayed his passage and he dropped soft-footed upon the terrace atop the

Gat Wharton opened his mouth to speak but words never issued from it.

portico roof. Wide French doors were closed, but presented no problem to the *Spider*. A few moments of silent work with a lock-pick and he glided inside, shut the doors behind him against the night. Tautly, he stood listening to a low murmur of voices. They were close at hand!

Wentworth's feet picked a silent way across the room, avoiding obstacles as if by instinct, and came to a half-open door through which he peered. He was looking into a child's room, at Yolanda Blanton seated on the side of a child's bed, her hand gently on the head of a boy. And the voice the *Spider* heard was—the boy saying his prayers!

Through long moments, Wentworth stood frozen there. Incredible that this woman, this mother could be the agent of murder and crime! And yet...Wentworth shook his head slowly. He had heard her no more than three hours before cry men on to kill; Ellen Mayfrew had said she was the mistress of Roger Holme...He stood there until Yolanda rose and the boy tumbled into bed and the woman walked from the nursery by another door. Then he followed. He found another door which led into a hallway. Peering out, he saw her walking side by side with a man whose silhouette was vaguely familiar. They turned into a second-floor sitting-room—and Wentworth hesitated.

He could not reconcile what he had seen with the facts he knew. Slowly, determination hardened the line of his jaw. There could be no turning back. He, himself, had seen how obedient Holme was to her slightest suggestion, had heard her cry the pack on to kill the assassin whom, according to Warton's confession, she had inspired to his crime! And Wentworth knew that she wore on her forehead the sign of the Cobra's Fangs! No, the *Spider* could not turn back from duty for mere sentimentality. He had never stayed his hand when his own loved ones were in deadly peril.

WITHOUT a sound, the Spider crept along the corridor. Just inside the door, Yolanda stood in the arms of the man who, Wentworth saw with surprise, was the same young Senate guard he had noticed before. Yolanda was speaking softly...

"I do love you, Carl," she said, "but I cannot leave with you. You don't understand, I..."

Wentworth's nicely calculated blow dropped the Senate guard in his tracks and he stood before Yolanda, gun in hand.

"Not a sound, Yolanda," he ordered quietly, "Your lover is not injured—*yet!*"

Yolanda's eyes flared wide and she swayed, but made no sound. She dropped on her knees and took the unconscious man's head in her arms.

"You will pay for this!" she whispered, her voice trembling with anger.

"But first," Wentworth interrupted softly, "perhaps you will pay in a measure. How would you like Carl to know—*what you wear on your forehead!*"

The woman's pallor increased. "Who are you?" she whispered. "You...*Ah!*" It was a strangled scream. She jumped to her feet, reeled backward. "You are...*the Spider!*"

The *Spider's* lipless smile gave her the answer and she pressed her fists hard against her thighs.

"Judge me if you must," she whispered, "but Carl Gresham is innocent of everything save loving me."

Wentworth's grimness did not relax. "Where is the temple of Siva?" he asked coldly. "Who gives you the orders you transmit to Holme and to the guards? Speak—or I may *judge* this Carl Gresham!" The *Spider's* gun snouted toward the unconscious man. If he were innocent as she said—and as Wentworth was inclined to believe—he was safe from the *Spider's* justice. But Yolanda could not know that. Her back was to the wall, her hands pressing against it for support.

"Have mercy!" she whispered. "Oh, have mercy! You do not understand. I dare not speak, or my son will be...*sacrificed to Siva!* Oh, have pity."

The footfall in the hallway was velvet soft, yet Wentworth's acutely listening ears caught it. He whirled. His gun blasted death through the darkened doorway. He saw a tall, turbaned man start to fall. An arm whipped around the man from behind and the body was pushed forward as a shield for the attackers. Wentworth laughed—and broke the arm with a bullet, squeezed off another as the body sagged and he had a clear shot at the man behind. Plainly, Yolanda, pressed against the wall, had sounded some signal. These were the hidden guards, but how many were there? Vague shadows of men moved in the dim hallway. If he attacked them…

The blow on his head was savagely violent. It drove him to his knees and fragments of pottery fell to the floor about him. For a moment, he had a crazy idea that his head had broken into shards. He fought to lift his guns with numbed hands and men poured in through the doorway and overwhelmed him.

Blows rained upon his shoulders and aching head. The guns were torn from him. He thought with difficulty, *"Subconsciously, I must have been fool enough to believe and trust Yolanda. I turned my back to her."*

His failing eyes saw the child bound through the doorway, face twisted in fright, heard Yolanda's voice, dimly.

"Sssh, darling, it's all right now," she soothed, then her voice turned cold. "That man is the *Spider!* Take him to the altar of Siva! It is a command!"

CHAPTER SEVEN
The Legions Of Siva

WENTWORTH did not wholly lose consciousness. He felt the bite of the ropes into his wrists, knew numbly that he was dragged from the house. The cooler airs of the night slowly revived him and he found himself wedged in the rear seat of a sedan between two Hindus who held long-bladed knives against his sides. The car was rolling steadily through Washington streets. A quick glance showed the course was southeast. Then Wentworth remembered. He was bound for the sacrificial altar of Siva the Terrible!

With small tentative movements, Wentworth tested the bonds about his wrists. They were cruelly tight. No slightest chance of working free. Even if he succeeded, those keen knives would plunge hilt-deep in his sides the instant he made a hostile move. Wentworth forced calmness on himself. He could only wait and hope. He blamed himself bitterly because of the capture, and…

The car ground to a halt as uniformed men darted out into the street. For a moment, hope sprang high in Wentworth's heart—until he recognized the men as Holme Guards! They carried flaming torches in their hands and there behind the trees, the red glare of fire brightened momentarily. A man was screaming, horribly. Violently, Wentworth's arms strained against his bonds. This was Indianois City all over again. Some of Holme's "boys" were growing too enthusiastic once more!

One of the guards leaned through the window and jabbed a burning torch at Wentworth's face, jumped back with a shrill laugh—and the car lurched on. Plainly, the Hindu driver had a pass. Under Wentworth's tightened lids, his eyes burned coldly. The torch had singed his hair, inflicted a minor burn on his cheek. But he had not flinched. Between the roadside trees, he glimpsed a burning house. Against a lawn tree, a man was being burned alive. A man...Why, good God—that was Senator Wida's house!

Wida's name had headed the list Wentworth had given Ram Singh. Either the Sikh had not been in time or Wida had refused to heed the warning. And so he was dying, terribly. Lord! If they dared to attack Wida, what other atrocities were at this moment being committed in Washington? This was the proscription the *Spider* had foreseen as the aftermath of what would be called a plot to assassinate Holme. Wentworth fought his bonds and a knife dug into his side.

"You will be quiet, *sahib*," one of the Hindus ordered.

The car rolled leisurely on and, ever and again, marching bands of the green-uniformed guards crossed their path and against the sky the red glare of fires rose luridly. For a while, Wentworth had dared hope that the police soon would crush out the lawlessness but when last a group of Holme men had passed, there had been police with them, carrying torches. Dazedly, Wentworth told himself it could not continue. Troops would be called out, but time dribbled past and there was no check upon the marauders. God, this was...was *revolution!* And a revolution led and mastered by criminals! No matter what Holme intended, he would be used by the criminals to loot the nation of its wealth. The plot was gigantic, incredible, the events like the macabre disasters of a nightmare—but they were taking place before Wentworth's very eyes.

Presently, the sedan drew to a halt beside a sweep of lawn before another home. The flare of torches was all about it. A hundred men were crowded about its doors. A long, triumphant shout lifted from them. The door was whipped open and a man was thrown out—a man clad in the long black robes of a judge. Satirically, the Holme Guard had dressed the man in his judicial dignity before they dragged him to humiliation and death. The man's hair was snow-white. Struggling to his feet, he was aged but cloaked in a dignity that should have given even these mad killers pause. With a low cry, Wentworth recognized the man. Justice McTavish, of the Supreme Court!

AFTER that one cry, Wentworth sat rigidly, waiting. His list given to Ram Singh had been damnably accurate. This was another whom the Spider had tried futilely to warn. Was Ram Singh, Wentworth wondered, anywhere near this place? If he were...Wentworth pursed his lips, and shrilly, piercing, a whistle rang out. It was shut off almost instantly by one of the Hindus, but if Ram Singh were within hearing he would have recognized a signal from his master. It was a forlorn hope, but Wentworth was in despair. It was one of the few times in his long life of battle with the forces of crime and underworld that hope had almost deserted him. Not that he would cease to fight, but it was so hopeless, so hopeless...

With somber eyes, Wentworth saw the judge dragged across the lawn, hooted at and belabored by the guardsmen. It had been McTavish's misfortune to tell a Senate committee that the thing the Senate proposed to do in enacting the bill for a Secretary of Audit and Finance was unconstitutional; and, especially, the method by which it proposed to appoint one of its own members to office if the President's nominees did not satisfy the Senate. With a start, Wentworth realized that Justice McTavish was being thrust directly toward this car. A few seconds later, the front door was jerked open and McTavish was shoved into the seat.

"To the altar of Siva!" the guards shouted. "Death to all enemies of the Sword of Justice!"

Justice McTavish indulged in no fulminations. He ignored his captors as totally as if they did not exist and sat bolt upright with his robes drawn in dignity about him. There was an ugly wound on the back of his head. His white hair was stained...For a while, as the car rolled slowly on, the shouting guards marched beside it. They began to chant, then to sing.

The aged justice's body was stretched out in the arms of the huge idol.

The tune was the Battle Hymn of the Republic but the words were desecration.

Under cover of the furor, Wentworth snapped out a crisp phrase in French: "Did any one warn you to flee, Judge?"

Justice McTavish turned his venerable head a moment after a blow had crushed Wentworth's lips. "No," the jurist said quietly, "no one warned me."

Harshly, McTavish was ordered to keep silent, but Wentworth had learned what he wished to know. Ram Singh might possibly have been near-by. It was a faint hope, but Wentworth was clutching at straws. He did not attempt to speak again and after seeming hours during which the madness of rebellion increased wantonly, the car halted before a decrepit building in a slattern tenement district. He was yanked from his seat and, with the justice, thrust violently into a stench-ridden hallway and down cellar stairs. A trap-door revealed still another basement and the acrid odor of stale incense was bitter in Wentworth's nostrils. He was not surprised when heavy portiéres were whipped aside and revealed the scene of which Gat Warton had babbled before he died.

What fairly stopped the breath in Wentworth's throat was the monstrous idol which filled one end of the chamber. Wentworth had seen various manifestations of Siva in a hundred Indies temples, but no such nightmare monster as this could be conceived. In general outline, the figure was conventional, but the face held a malignancy that stirred revulsion and rage deep in the soul. Even more horrible were the six visible arms of the god. As if they, too, were deadly snakes, they twined in sinuous convolutions and the bronze hands plucked and plucked again at the altar beneath its knees!

It was only when he pulled his blazing eyes away from the last hideous detail that he became aware of the woman in priestess robes who stood beside the idol. His breath hissed between his teeth as he recognized the pallid features. Not Yolanda; her he could have understood, but...but *Ellen Mayfrew!* Though she must have recognized him in his *Spider's* garb, though she was a personal friend of Justice McTavish, Ellen gave no sign of knowing either of them. Her lips moved and gradually silence gradually fell save for her voice which soared in an outlandish chant. Even the restless arms of the idol fell into the conventional pose of Siva and remained still. But there was a quiver, a waiting in that stillness—and once a hand quested...*hungrily*...across the bare altar!

Men's hands closed on Wentworth's arms, and he felt the ropes sliced from his wrists! For a moment, he thought some hidden friend had done it, but all too soon he recognized his error. The men who held Justice McTavish hurled him to the floor and ripped the clothing from his aged body. Within a space of seconds, he had been laid upon that awful altar and the hands...the hands of Siva were upon him!

WENTWORTH understood then why his hands had been freed and a shout of rage beat against his clenched teeth. Four of the hands of Siva had fastened upon McTavish, each by a separate wrist or ankle, and were lifting the sagging body. It seemed a gentle thing at first, the way in which those four hands raised the aged justice—but only at first. Then the arms bowed out, and McTavish's body no longer sagged. It was stretched out rigidly in the torture rack of those bronze hands. Stringy muscles bulged hideously in the man's body and a weak moan was squeezed from his bitten lips.

"In this way," lifted the clear, changing voice of Ellen Mayfrew, "shall the enemies of the Sword ever perish!"

"Ellen!" Wentworth cried. "In Heaven's name, Ellen, stop this thing!"

A brutal hand struck Wentworth savagely across the mouth. His muscles corded with fury. He tried to contain himself. Against so many, he could do nothing—especially without arms. And the idol's grip on McTavish had relaxed a little. The emaciated body swung gently to and fro—and one of the hands began to twist McTavish's right foot outward and back, slowly, with exquisite care. The ankle gave first. McTavish gasped. When the hip broke with a dull cracking, McTavish screamed and his head rolled limply. Gently, he was lowered to the altar. The hands hovered over him and the eyes—Great God, was that horrid idol *alive!* They were, were alive. Wentworth could swear to it. Alive and watching the helpless man with the glistening cruelty of a cat!

Wentworth forced his gaze away from the torture and furtively scanned the chamber. The walls were barren stone save where scarlet portiéres were hung and here and there an arched doorway opened a black mouth. Shaven-headed priests in yellow robes lined the walls. Only two men held Wentworth but, naked to the waist, they were powerfully muscled and their hands did not for a moment relax their hold.

Only one thing was favorable. His guards' eyes were greedily on the altar. If the *Spider* could escape these two...But what, without weapons, could he do against so many? His gaze narrowed. There were weapons! Knives at the belts of his guards and there, beside the altar, was a length of heavy chain with an iron manacle at its end. And now was the moment when he must strike; now when once more McTavish feebly stirred and those torturing hands waited to pounce! Gently, Wentworth swayed toward the men on his right. The guard on his left tightened his grip, tugged. For an instant, Wentworth resisted—until the pull became almost irresistible. But because in his own body, he absorbed the strain, the Hindu on his right was not aware of this silent struggle. He became aware of it violently. Wentworth abruptly relaxed his opposition to the pull toward his left. He threw his entire weight in that direction. As he had foreseen, the sudden jerk of the Hindu on his left, plus his own strength, wrenched him free of the man on his right.

Wentworth did not move blindly. As he catapulted against the Hindu to his right, Wentworth sprang from the floor and drove the crown of his head into the man's jaw! At the same instant, his freed right hand closed on the man's knife and yanked it free. There was no need to use the blade on its owner. Under the impact of Wentworth's head, bones had cracked. The Hindu spilled to the floor and, quick as a black panther, Wentworth spun and threw his captured knife at the other guard—dove in behind it. He saw the weapon drive home to the hilt in the man's chest. Almost as quickly as the flung knife, Wentworth had reached the man. A snatch, a wrench and with a long, curved blade in each hand Wentworth was springing toward the altar!

So rapidly had Wentworth's attack begun and finished that the chant of the priests of Siva had barely changed into a hoarse, many-tongued cry of alarm when the *Spider* was racing toward the idol. Quick as he was, one other thing was faster—the six arms of Siva! Wentworth was still three long strides from the altar when McTavish was snatched high into the air by those torturing hands. Wentworth hurled a knife straight at the glittering eyes. There was a ringing clash of metal on metal, and the knife fell to the floor, unblooded. The thing was mechanical then. Of course. He must stop that monstrous machine...

The priests' cries had changed to anger. Screaming curses, the yellow-robed men were flying to the attack with knives flashing in their hands. Wentworth caught up the chain, sprang wide about the idol's figure. He scarcely glanced toward Ellen, but he was aware of her wide gaze upon him, conscious, too, of the horror in her eyes. Then he was in the shadow of Siva. Another bronze arm attached to the thing's back made a lightning grab for Wentworth, but he eluded it, dodged back while he searched for some vulnerable spot to strike. There was none. The smooth, impregnable body of Siva was a seamless fortress. In its torturing hands, Justice McTavish screamed—and its sound pierced even above the angry clamor of the priests!

A movement caught the corner of Wentworth's eyes and his head jerked about toward Ellen Mayfrew. In her hand was a small automatic! Wentworth cursed savagely, but even as he leaped to wrest the weapon from her, Ellen tossed it toward him. Her face was drawn and pale, but otherwise without expression. In her eyes was a pleading…Then she was blotted out in the swirl of attacking yellow robes!

With a savage swing, Wentworth whirled the heavy manacle chain like a mace. It crushed a man's skull, sliced across the face of another, snapped a reaching, knife arm. Wentworth had thrust the automatic into his belt for ultimate use. It would hold only a few bullets at best, and here were many priests. His left hand gripped, instead, the knife. As a priest dropped to his knees and lunged forward beneath the flail, Wentworth side-stepped lightly and slashed downward with the blade. His aim was true. The edge grated on bone in the back of the man's neck. He dropped, quivering, on his face.

Of the six who had struck at him in the first mad rush of men, four already were out of the fight. Wentworth did not wait for the other two to attack. He leaped forward, swinging the deadly chain. A knife flickered toward him and he ducked barely in time. Another leap and he was upon the two priests. The chain finished one, the knife the other and for a moment Wentworth was clear. There were still fully twenty of the yellow robes clamoring toward him and others streaming from the black mouths of the doorways. Hopeless this fight, but it was never the *Spider's* way to surrender. His eyes flew over the room and then, slowly, a smile crept to his lips. The room was lighted by electricity. Undoubtedly, the idol was, too.

In a half dozen long strides, he had reached the nearest of the lights. Gripping the knife in a fold of his robe, he pried into the bracket. At the flash of blue-white light, he laughed—and the laughter echoed across the vault of this underground room, flat and mocking in the darkness, the laughter of the *Spider*. As the last glimmer of light faded, Wentworth glimpsed in the mouth of a doorway, a tall and strongly built Hindu who did not wear the robe, whose face was hidden in the bushy mask of a beard, and who carried a heavy automatic in each hand. Even as darkness fell, those guns began to blast and once more Wentworth laughed.

In French, he cried out across the turmoil, "*A moi*, Ram Singh! To me—I climb the idol!"

Three points of light remained in the room, three censers which glowed redly and sent up fogs of swirling incense smoke. Two of these were immediately before the idol of Siva and by their upward thrown glare, he could see that the arms of Siva were motionless, that McTavish dangled limply in their hold. With a running leap, Wentworth reached the lowest of the arms and climbed rapidly to the head. He had confirmed his guess. The thing operated by electricity. With Ram Singh and his two mighty guns, they might yet win clear and smash this hellish cult.

Straddling the shoulders of the giant idol, Wentworth cupped his hands and began to boom out words in Hindustani.

"Fools!" he cried. "Sons of monkeys! Siva fights on the side of the strong! Flee, ye who call yourselves my priests. Weaklings! Filthy animals of the lowest caste! Flee, lest I destroy you all!"

Frightened cries burst from the yellow robes. Ram Singh's guns were momentarily silenced, and presently Wentworth was aware of a dark figure that clambered toward him.

"*Wah, sahib!*" whispered the strong, nasal voice of Ram Singh. "If I were not a Sikh and a Singh, a worshiper of the one true God, you had frightened me with your voice of Siva!"

In the darkness, Wentworth smiled. "Your guns, warrior!" he whispered. "Do you free the man from Siva's hands." The automatics lay sweetly in his palms. He laughed sharply and began a deliberate fire. He knew where were the doorways that arched into this underworld hell and his bullets sped unerringly into their mouths. And the shrieks of men answered him.

But light was growing in the room and to Wentworth's nostrils came the stench of burnt rubber. He twisted his head about and cursed softly. From the light-connection where his knife had blown out the fuses, flames were beginning to lick toward the ceiling. A wooden beam ran upward there. The floor overhead was wood. Within minutes, the dry, ancient timbers were blazing. Ram Singh was back beside him, standing upon one of the motionless arms.

"I cannot free the *sahib*," he said gravely, "but there is no need. His head has been...twisted off. On my head be the blame, master, that I did not enter sooner. Thy servant heard thy signal and followed, but it was necessary to remove a few of these shaveling dogs from my path."

Wentworth's lips were drawn thinly. His guns cracked and cracked again as man after man paid for the enormity that had been committed here. Soon, he would have to flee. The smoke and fumes were thick, close to the ceiling where they crouched. Heat, too, was oppressive.

"What is written will be," he told Ram Singh quietly. "What could be done, you have done. Did you see aught to indicate who might be the leader of this rabble? The upper floors, what of them?"

"Empty...now, *sahib*." Ram Singh's teeth gleamed whitely through his beard. "Leader I saw none, but a woman fled as thy entered."

Wentworth shook his head violently. Nothing fitted in this damnable maze of death and horror. He would have staked his soul on the integrity of Ellen Mayfrew, on her sincerity...An abrupt thought made his lips shut bitterly. Was it Possible that Mayfrew's death had been a...fake? His examination of the fallen senator had been hurried in the extreme and before this criminals had hidden behind a mask of faked death. God, this heat! He must get out of here!

WENTWORTH stood upon the head of the idol and could lay his hands flat upon the flooring above. With his knife, he worked rapidly, then Ram Singh clambered up beside him and lent his mighty strength. Boards were ripped loose and presently, with a leap, Wentworth seized the edge of the opening and muscled himself upward, Ram Singh just behind. Already, flames had reached into this cellar space. They fled through rooms empty save for themselves, broke finally through to the street. Of all the yellow priests who had swarmed to the temple-room, not one was visible now.

Wentworth's hand went warmly to Ram Singh's shoulder. "Between us, we have struck a blow at the Cobra tonight," he said strongly. "Perhaps, we have wiped out their nest and most of their men. Now, we only need find the head of this conspiracy..."

Ram Singh's face was gloomy. "Would that it were so, Master," he said harshly. "To find the chieftain is not enough. The city swarms with marching men as with vermin! Everywhere, they burn and destroy! Of the men you sent me to warn, not a single one escaped though several tried. They were hanged, burned, thrown into prisons. Fifteen men have I seen die tonight at the hands of these guardsmen in green!"

The news drove the blood from Wentworth's face. Some part of all this he had guessed, but that the defeat had been so sweeping he could not dream. He shook his head, strode toward the car Ram Singh had parked nearby.

"It cannot last!" he said violently. "When the country learns what has happened here, the people will rise against such slaughter, such lawlessness..." A thought stopped his words in his throat. Abruptly, he switched on the radio, and a news commentator's voice spoke briskly:

"The conspiracy to assassinate Roger

Holme involved men in high places," he said. "Tonight, every one of those men has been arrested or has received the just deserts of his infamy at the hands of outraged citizens. Many, facing exposure, committed suicide, rather than face the punishment they earned..."

A harsh oath rasped from Wentworth's lips. If the radio could twist the rioting and murder he had seen tonight into a just expiation of crimes...But, damn it, there had been no conspiracy to murder Holme! It had been a frame-up from first to last, a deliberate move to permit such wholesale murders as had been committed this night. However, an armed force of men could easily subdue the radio broadcasting service. Surely, the newspapers...

From a drugstore phone booth, Wentworth urgently called an editor friend on a newspaper. A harsh voice answered. "Harper committed suicide early tonight," it said. "This paper is now in the hands of loyal men."

"Loyal to whom?" Wentworth snapped.

The man's voice became a chant, "To the most high, to the chief of the multitude, to the sword of unalterable justice..."

Wentworth hung up savagely and his car was no more than a block away when other machines slammed to the curb and a squad of green-uniformed Holme Guards stormed into the drugstore. Wentworth had no need to ask why they were there—and he read a further dread meaning into their presence. To have traced that call so quickly, the Holme Guards must have complete dominance also over telephonic communications!

What chance had the people of the United States to learn the truth of this dastardly conspiracy if all the channels of free speech and public information were controlled and censored by these fanatic clansmen of Senator Holme! What did his petty victory, his vengeance upon a few shaveling priests of an awful god amount to in the face of this calamity?

Abruptly, the street ahead of him filled with storm troopers and behind him, he heard the racing motors of other cars. Already, the men who had sought him at the drugstore were on his trail. He bore the accelerator to the floor, tossed a gun into Ram Singh's lap. These men might be guilty only of hero-worship, but the hero they adored was a beast. And their hands were stained with murder blood this night. No longer would the *Spider* hold his hand from them.

As Ram Singh began a deliberate fire and the charging car slammed the first Holme Guard from his path, Wentworth knew suddenly that his only chance of living to crush this conspiracy lay in flight. Holme owned Washington and the campaign against him must be waged from without. But God alone knew whether the *Spider* would succeed in escaping from a city where every street vomited its hordes of murdering storm troopers—storm troopers of the Sword of Justice! Wentworth's cold, mocking laughter rolled out in the wake of his bullets.

CHAPTER EIGHT
A Forlorn Hope Fails

MEN flung themselves from the path of the Spider's onrushing juggernaut, but guns blasted in their hands. The window beside Wentworth crashed in upon him, gashed his hand. Wentworth's gun answered and the roar of Ram Singh's automatic beside him beat out a rhythm of death. Behind them, Wentworth could no longer hear pursuing cars, but their lights were blindingly bright against the bullet-pocked windshield. A tire blew out with a hissing explosion and the car swerved violently, rocketed on.

They had swept through the first ambuscade, but that punctured tire doomed flight. A phalanx of storm troopers had taken the road behind, following at a jog-trot. Presently, even above the crazy racket of the flat tire, Wentworth could hear their rising chant. And the pursuing cars bore down on them. Bullets whanged into the body of the sedan. The windshield went out and, abruptly, the engine began to sputter.

Ram Singh turned his head and his teeth were shining white. "*Wah, sahib*, it seems thy servant and thou must fight!" His voice was calm, deep. He was deliberately thumbing fresh cartridges into two clips for his automatic, then performing a like service for Wentworth. "Do thou flee, master. Thy servant will hold back these dogs."

Wentworth shook his head sharply. "Not necessary," he said curtly. "When one of their cars comes close, I will kill the driver and we will have a fresh chance. If you fire at them, keep your bullets high!"

Ram Singh chuckled and, softly, his nasal voice began to chant a war song of his people. It was a wild and stirring thing. Wentworth felt his blood pulse to its beat...The pursuing cars were very close now, two of them. They had ceased firing, apparently certain of their prey.

"The second car, Ram Singh," Wentworth said quietly. "Kill the driver."

The song was still on Ram Singh's lips. It cut off for an instant punctuated by a double blast of his automatic, then picked up again, louder than before. One set of headlights behind skittered crazily across the road, illuminated a tree. The shadows sprang out strong and black and then it was all shadow as the lights crashed out. A man began to scream before the echoes died out behind them. The shooting from the pursuers began again in a savage flurry. Wentworth released the wheel of the car and let it wobble wildly. It hurtled the curb. He swung it wide of a tree that loomed in their path, whirled the car broadside into a skid that set it teetering on two wheels.

"Out!" Wentworth rapped at Ram Singh.

The Sikh dived through his door, rolled clear just as the car toppled over. Wentworth screamed hoarsely and kept on screaming. Brakes squealed thirty feet away at the curbing and men began to run. Wentworth made his screams weaker, let them fade out in a moan and he stood to peer out his broken window. Four men were running headlong toward the wreck, guns in hand.

"I hope they aren't dead!" one man shouted. "We'll burn them in the wreck!"

A thin smile twisted Wentworth's lips. He lined his sights on the man who shouted. As he squeezed the trigger, Ram Singh opened fire...In a few seconds, silence fell again on the empty street into which stole dimly the chant of the storm troopers who pursued on foot.

"Get that car started," Wentworth snapped at Ram Singh. He, himself, hesitated beside one of the dead and when he ran after the striding Sikh, he left behind a message for the Holme Guard who would follow—a message they could not fail to read, the seal of the *Spider!*

Moments later, they were racing northward through the city. No way of telling how far the Holme Guard sphere of influence extended. They would have to take back roads, avoid the cities in their path. Under his breath, Wentworth swore softly. He had called this rebellion. It was revolution, a successful revolt against the government! Not that Senator Holme would call it by any such name. But it was revolution, as complete and more bloody than Fascists had staged in Europe!

THROUGHOUT the dark hours of the night, they roared down the back roads. Three times, they were fired on and after the last attack Wentworth was forced to do all the driving. Ram Singh had taken a bullet through the flesh of his shoulder. Only the headlong speed at which they drove had saved them from more serious casualty. Dawn was grey in the East when finally they dared halt and eat. Cautiously, Wentworth put through a phone call for Nita.

It seemed incredible that her voice could still fall so gently on his ear after these hours of death and defeat. It had been so short a while since she had called him last, so short a while—but in the interim a country had fallen! Wentworth pulled himself up. He must not exaggerate. There was danger, but so far only Washington had succumbed, and the rebels could be overthrown.

For a moment when Nita's voice reached him, Wentworth bent his forehead against the wall and trembled; for another moment, he whispered his love to her—then his voice turned brisk. Swiftly, he outlined what he knew of the night's terror in Washington.

"See if you can get some of it in the newspapers," he told her. "They almost certainly

ROGER HOLME

YOLANDA

ELLIAS GODLOVE

have nothing but lies. Get hold of Commissioner Kirkpatrick, of the police, tell him what has happened. Tell him I'm on my way back and that I am afraid of a successful revolution by these criminals. Ask him to call a conference—I'll give you names in a moment—and have them all in his office by noon. That's all, dear, except—the criminals know me, yes. Be on your guard."

It was half-past eleven when Wentworth sped down the broad avenue toward Holland Tunnel and the final swoop under the Hudson river. He saw men run hurriedly, saw cars broadside across the entrance. With a curse, he spun the car in a U-turn and raced back against traffic on the one-way street. The Holme Guard was ahead of him, forewarned. God grant that his telephone call had not been overheard! But probably, they were watching for the *Spider* to return to New York. That was all.

Down a sidestreet, Wentworth raced and, short of the corner, stopped. They went on foot, then, were lucky enough to find a taxi. They changed twice in a swift reversal of direction, and in the end, caught a ferry.

"You go straight to Miss Nita," Wentworth instructed. "It's possible our telephone call was overheard. If it was, there will be a trap at police headquarters. Tell the *missie sahib* that. Tell her that there may be a trap for the entire conference and that I will have no more chance to communicate. It's up to her."

Ram Singh touched hands to forehead in a low salaam. *"Han, sahib,"* he acknowledged. "It is an order." But his eyes burned in fierce regret. Wentworth smiled and touched his shoulder briefly. "I think you will find battle with the *missie sahib*, also."

At the wharf, he parted from Ram Singh and sped in a taxi to police headquarters. It was already after twelve. The chase in Jersey City had cost him precious time. His eyes flashed keenly about him. No way of knowing yet whether his plans had been overheard or it was as he had guessed—that they had laid an ambuscade for a returning *Spider*. The attack came as he swung to the pavement before police headquarters and paid off the taxi driver. A car swung around the corner on squealing tires and guns began to blast instantly.

Wentworth flung flat on his belly on the pavement, guns in hand. He fired twice and the driver of the murder car arched backward over his seat, screaming. The car had not quite completed the turn and it swung wildly, glanced off a lamp post and charged a wall head-on. There was a crash, a jangle of broken glass—and silence. It was broken by the roar of the taxi motor as the man ran for it. Wentworth got up heavily from the pavement, walked stiff-kneed into police headquarters. His weariness was upon him and a great fear. This attack spelled only one thing. His plan had been overheard. And Nita—what of her? Had they allowed her to carry out his orders, or had they...

WENTWORTH'S pace quickened. He took the stairs to the second floor in long strides—jerking a phrase over his shoulder at the men who bolted for the street door. They knew Wentworth here, knew him for a close friend of Stanley Kirkpatrick, Commissioner of Police. As he reached the head of the steps, he saw Kirkpatrick, himself, swing out of his doorway, gun in hand. When he spotted Wentworth, he dropped back on his heels and slowly bolstered the long-barreled revolver.

"Thank God, Dick!" he cried. "When I heard that shooting, and knew you were late, I was worried."

Wentworth strode toward him, clasped his hand while he smiled faintly into the saturnine face of his friend. "Then you got the message from Nita?" he demanded rapidly. "Nita is...safe?"

Kirkpatrick nodded grimly. "Safe, yes, as a cordon on my picked men can make her! We have a Holme Guard in New York. I've dispersed fully a dozen meetings since last night." He knuckled his waxed military mustache, an invariable gesture when he was deeply worried. "The men are waiting." he said crisply.

They presented a strange contrast, those two as they strode back into the conference-room. Kirkpatrick, dapperly dressed as always, even to the gardenia on his lapel; Wentworth worn and unshaven, his eyes gleaming from a drawn face. But one thing sat upon them both like an accolade, confidence and ability. They

RASS MENLI

ELLEN MAYFREW

DANIEL BOROUGH

were men to command.

Kirkpatrick said briefly, "Mr. Wentworth, gentlemen. You know him by reputation. He was almost assassinated at the door."

Wentworth nodded, looked slowly over the faces about the long table. These were men who controlled the news facilities of the country, telegraph and telephones, radio, newspapers; all of them were wealthy and powerful. If they accepted his story, and opposed Holme, the revolution could be beaten. If they allowed the rigid censorship that obtained in Washington to be clapped on here—the country was lost.

"Gentlemen," Wentworth began quietly, "armed men seized the government of the United States last night!"

Shocked incredulity marked their faces when he began but as Wentworth talked and narrated incident after incident in the brisk, detailed style he could use so effectively, disbelief gave way to grave concern; to frantic worry.

"You gentlemen can defeat this," Wentworth concluded crisply. "If your newspapers, your wire services, your radio broadcasts tell the truth of what has happened in Washington, no Holme Guard will dare show his face on the street. Commissioner Kirkpatrick will give you every protection in his power." He smiled grimly. "I have carried my message to Garcia. It is up to you gentlemen to spread that message over the country—and without delay. I am going back to Washington within a few hours, carrying help I hope. I am going to try desperately to reach the President.

"So far, I am sure they have not dared to do more than circumscribe him. If he can appeal to the governors of the states—and you lay the groundwork with your broadcast of the facts—we will smash this revolution before it can spread. Will you give your help?"

For moments after Wentworth ceased to speak, there was absolute silence in the long conference hall. The president of a national radio system was the first to rise.

"My stations will do all in their power. I request protection, Mr. Commissioner. As soon as that is assured, we'll begin broadcasting. Mr. Wentworth, if you could repeat your story on a national hook-up, it would help."

A newspaper publisher jumped up. "Same here," he snapped. "Let's get some fast action. I've been printing lies. Lies! That was all they gave me from Washington."

In a few minutes, every man there had pledged his help. Wentworth felt a warm, expansive glow in his breast. By heavens, it took more than an armed uprising—no matter how cleverly planned—to overthrow the power of the government. The people were stauch and when they knew the truth, they would act—as these men would act. He had despaired too soon. Nothing could stop them...

The simultaneous crash on the doors which opened from three sides of the room was like a blast of cannon in the confined space. And it was overwhelmingly effective. The three doors were blown wide open. In the three doorways stood men with machine guns. Behind them, in a thick phalanx, were rank on rank of men in green uniforms, men of the Holme Guard!

From the main entrance, a single lean man strode forward, glaring at them dourly—Elias Godlove!

"You are all under arrest," he said, his voice rasping out, twanging nasally. "The charge is conspiring against the United States Government. Treason, gentlemen!"

Commissioner Kirkpatrick stepped forward to confront him. "You are a fool," he said curtly, calmly. "Your men are without authority. You are criminals, bearing arms without warrant. You men throw down those weapons or you'll spend the rest of your lives in prison. Disarm, I say!"

Such was the force of Kirkpatrick's personality, that a number of the men were visibly shaken. One or two gun muzzles wavered, but Elias Godlove laughed harshly.

"Sorry to contradict you, Kirkpatrick," he said, sneering. "These men are the United States Police Force, authorized by the Congress within the last hour. Each one of them has the full right to bear arms, to make arrests anywhere in the United States or its territories for offenses against the government."

"Impossible," Wentworth whispered, but he knew it was possible. Opposition had been shattered by the wholesale murders of last night. The remaining legislators would obey slavishly, in fear of their very lives.

Godlove drew himself up sternly. "Once more, gentlemen, I call on you to surrender without show of force. I should regret"—he smiled and his teeth were jagged as a wolf's—"I should regret very much having to overpower resistance. I'm afraid not one of you would survive an order to…open fire!"

ALREADY the fortunes of the nation had seemed at utmost ebb, but this, Wentworth realized, was complete defeat. Not only was Holme paramount in Washington, but, his power reached out and throttled New York. Without question, press and radio, all communications systems, were being seized similarly throughout the country. And those men in this room, the capitalists who alone might be strong enough to fight off the strangle-hold on liberty, were helpless prisoners.

Frantically, Wentworth sought a way out—but there was none. At the first hostile movement, those ready machine guns would blast from three sides. Then, truly, there would be a death of hope!

"You will deposit all arms on the table." Godlove ordered harshly. "Any man who retains a weapon will be executed later. If one of you resists—you all die now! Wentworth, Kirkpatrick, you two first."

There seemed no choice.

"Quickly, now," Godlove fumed. "I am going to wait no longer. Here and now you will surrender—or die!"

For a mad moment, Wentworth considered his chances of killing Godlove. He might succeed, but the man stood too far away to be taken as hostage. And his death alone would be futile. With heavy movements, Wentworth drew his guns and laid them on the table. Kirkpatrick obeyed more obstinately, and only one other of the captives was armed. Immediately, Godlove had them marching in single-file from the conference-room by the main door, Wentworth and Kirkpatrick first. As they moved out, the ranks of Holme Guards split, but the machine guns did not waver and bayonets confronted them.

Through the antechamber, where more machine guns kept hungry watch toward the hall door. And there, too, the muzzles of the deadly rapid-fire guns showed. There was a weary droop to the shoulders of Kirkpatrick. Wentworth imitated his movements. He had not given up hope—but only because despair could find no room in his brave heart. He had warned Nita there might be an ambuscade, against such force as this she would be helpless.

Beyond the hall door, the file of prisoners turned right. Wentworth stepped out—and the door whipped shut.

"Flat on your face, Dick!" a voice gasped—and the voice was Nita's!

Wentworth did not delay to speculate. He pitched forward and carried Kirkpatrick with him, and over their heads machine guns chattered savagely! It was only when he had rolled clear of the door, when he heard the answering thunder of guns from within that Wentworth could see what had happened. A half dozen storm troopers were sprawled unconscious on the floor and still in the air he could sniff the traces of a strange odor—by the heavens, he knew it now! A soporific gas of which he had only a scanty store left since the wreckage of his apartment fort in a recent battle with criminals! A shout of triumph rose in his throat. Flat against the wall, he sprang erect. On each side of the door, Nita and Ram Singh crouched, firing through the barrier with short deadly bursts.

"The bombs, Dick!" Nita cried.

Wentworth then saw a canvas bag beside her feet. With a quick leap, he had it opened and hurled four of the glass shells through the shattered door glass into the room beyond. Four—and there were no more. He straightened beside Nita, took the machine gun from her hands, rapidly snapped on a fresh drum of ammunition and took up the work. Beside him, Nita stood straight and still, her face deadly pale in spite of the smile on her lips.

Suddenly, Wentworth was laughing and the sound was gay, triumphant. How could the men of Holme and Godlove defeat him when there was faith and loyalty such as this on the opposite side. He bent toward Nita—the sounds of resistance within were dying—and brushed her cheek with his lips.

"Hurry now, darling," he cried. "Tell Kirkpatrick to take what men he can rely on and hustle everyone from the conference into hiding. You go with them."

Nita's hand rested on his arm. "I'll tell Kirkpatrick," she said, "but I'm coming back to you. And I'm going to Washington when you go. I've joined the auxiliary of the Holme Guard!"

"You can't!" Wentworth said violently. "This is only a skirmish. The Holme Guard controls every newspaper and radio station in the city! We've got to fly!"

Nita smiled faintly, "I'll be back!"

Only three guns fired spasmodically from within. Wentworth held his machine gun ready and gestured to Ram Singh.

"Follow the *missie sahib*," he said curtly, "See that she goes to safety with Kirkpatrick."

Ram Singh's eyes met those of his master and slowly he shook his head. "Master, I stay by thee!"

Wentworth's eyes bore on those of the Sikh, scornfully. "Is thy master such a weakling then that he needs a nurse? Is he so badly served, then? Go, and be her safety on thy head!"

Ram Singh's eyes dropped. He salaamed low and saluted. "My head, master!" He started down the corridor at a swift run, and Wentworth drew in his breath softly. One thing remained to be done and then, he, too, would flee. Godlove must die!

WENTWORTH held his machine gun ready before him, peered into the silent room—and a curse leaped to his lips. The inner doors were tightly shut. Only the outer guard had fallen before bullets and bombs. And in the conference room were Godlove and fully a dozen men! Even as Wentworth recognized that fact, the inner doors whirled open and guns began to speak. Wentworth flinched back, squeezed off short bursts of shots, but he must retreat. There was no other course. Not enough of the gas remained even in that close inner room to overcome the men. Here in the drafty hall, there was none at all. If he had more ammunition, he might still remain and fight it out, but he had barely a half drum left...

Slowly, Wentworth backed up the hall, in the opposite direction to that down which the others had fled. There was a narrow stairway here and, from its head, he could still command the doorway—as long as his bullets lasted. He crouched to rip automatics from the holsters of two of the unconscious guards; then turned and ran.

He was within a stride of the stairs when a gun crashed deafeningly behind him. Wentworth felt the blow and it hammered him to his knees. Deliberately, he pitched forward to the protection of the steps, fell halfway down before he could catch himself. His brain still flashed with lightning clarity, but his body was

NITA VAN SLOAN

slow and fumbling in its response. It seemed to take minutes to get to his feet, to face up the stairs and lie his length upon them. He rested the machine gun in the corner between newel-post and floor, squeezed on the trigger. There could be no aiming. His left arm was entirely helpless and an agony spread across his back. Numbness was creeping up his spine toward his brain.

The gun was empty, presently. Wentworth hooked his right arm across the bannister and used that support to slide down. He had an automatic in his right hand, but there was a haze before his eyes. Ahead of him, a man's body loomed and Wentworth tried to lift his gun. There was a single recoil which he felt more than heard, then arms were about him—strong arms that lifted and bore him downward into a darkness that reached up to welcome him.

IT WAS a long while before Wentworth's eyes knew once more the dingy light of day; before he knew that Nita and Ram Singh had disobeyed his orders. It was, to be precise, three weeks. And on the day when, in the slums refuge to which Nita had carried him, he became aware once more of life and living, Nita left him for Washington.

"You've plenty of time to get your strength back," Nita told him quietly. "Holme completely owns the country. The only way he and his thieving murderers will ever be put out is by a long battle of propaganda and, in the end, a counter-revolution. I'm going to Washington to learn what I can and to send out the facts. Kirkpatrick and a few of the others escaped to Mexico and they're setting up a broadcasting station there and a printing shop. I'll come back to you when I can, Dick."

Wentworth's hand reached out for her and its feebleness dismayed him. "It's no woman's battle, dear," he said, as firmly as he could. "You stay here. I have a way, too, of getting back into Washington. In a few days..."

"Not in a few weeks!" Nita told him flatly. "That bullet broke your shoulder blade, went through your lung and missed your heart by inches. God knows how you survived. Oh, Dick..."

Nita dropped on her knees beside his bed, head buried against his shoulder and his fingers toyed with the chestnut curls that clustered about her nape. Presently, the sleep of great weakness overwhelmed him and when he awoke again, Nita was gone. The weeks that dragged past were misery. There was nothing in the newspapers that might give him a clue to actual happenings in Washington; and no news from Nita. She could not write lest she betray them both. It was a month to the day after she left that Wentworth drove his weakened body from bed. Two days later, in the absence of Ram Singh's grim-kept guard, Wentworth slipped from the house and made his feeble way to one spot his enemies had never found—the slattern room of one Blinky McQuade.

There was no such person as Blinky McQuade—except as he existed in Richard Wentworth. But the underworld knew Blinky well—a safe-blower who had been almost blinded by a blast and had become, consequently, an expert cracksman. Every criminal dive was open to him. They understood his long absences, for his deftness was needed by out-of-town crooks on tough jobs occasionally.

Nevertheless, Wentworth entered the sanctuary on Holian Alley furtively by the back court that opened also on Pallin Place. The touch of his attenuated fingers opened a secret panel in the massive head of the bed and, within a few moments, it was no longer Wentworth who occupied the room, but a shambling taut-faced man with a strongly arched nose and eyes that blinked weakly behind hooded spectacles. And in Blinky, no man would recognize Richard Wentworth, wealthy clubman and sometime dabbler in criminology!

In the days that followed, Blinky McQuade rested much and labored rarely—but when he worked some safe of extraordinary difficulty was burglarized and the newspapers printed the stories of the thefts. And the underworld looked on him with respect. They knew whose hand had the skill for those enterprises, though police had never been able to prove a thing against Blinky McQuade. It was ten days before Wentworth's campaign bore fruit but at the end of that time, the furtive grapevine of the underworld brought him the word he sought. There was work for him, at incredible wages, in Washington—in the ranks of the Holme Guard!

The major of the Holme Guard before whom Blinky McQuade was ushered in Washington had once been the head of a white-slavery racket in New York city—a man notable as an organizer and well known to the *Spider*. The major smiled thinly at Wentworth.

"Three hundred a week," he said curtly. "There's a job to pull off tonight. You'll get five thousand for that—if you succeed."

Blinky McQuade was impressed. "Cripes!" he exclaimed. "How long has this been going on!"

The major leaned forward and smiled—unpleasantly. "Long enough, Blinky, to figure ways to punish those who fail! We have some Hindu friends who are clever at torture—but that's only for those who fail. For those who succeed there's more money than you ever saw before, Blinky! Come back here at nine o'clock, without fail."

It was obvious that Blinky was completely intimidated. He was shaking as he left. How could the major guess it was with rage! These men were supposed to be government police and Blinky, cracksman, would be paid for crime with government money by a major who was notorious for one of the filthiest criminal ventures known! His anger left him weak, for he was far from having recouped his lithe strength. But he drove himself stubbornly on. He had to learn how matters stood in Washington, had to figure out the details of the plan that had come to him in his long weeks of illness.

WENTWORTH spent an hour in making sure he was not followed; it took three quarters of an hour more to rent a car and to find where, among the ranks of the Holme Auxiliary, Nita was employed. The uniform the major had given Blinky permitted him to inquire. Wentworth announced to the office manager where Nita worked that Nita was wanted at "headquarters." Nita gave no sign of recognition, but calmly delayed to adjust the pert uniform cap on her curls before she left with Wentworth. Neither spoke until they were in the car, then Nita's hand only clenched on Wentworth's.

"Oh my dear, my dear!" she whispered. "I thought those beasts had found you!"

Wentworth made no reply, but his lips were twisted as he drove off—toward headquarters, in case of watchers. Everywhere, eyes would be upon them. There could be no more greeting than this between them. His fingers twined and twined again with hers.

"You're...not strong, Dick," Nita said quietly. "You should be resting, recovering your strength. And how did you get the uniform?"

"Don't waste time, dear," Wentworth told her gently. "I must know so many things, and you'll have to be back soon."

Nita drew in a slow breath, glanced about carefully as they rolled through the streets, then began to talk rapidly. "No use telling you the thousand crimes that have been committed in the name of justice. Kirkpatrick has broadcast them from Mexico, but it's death to be caught listening, or reading one of his pamphlets. The Senate is preparing to impeach the President on some ridiculous trumped-up charges..."

Wentworth uttered an angry curse. "They can't get away with that!"

Nita smiled slightly. "Oh, can't they? Every member of the Senate is under Holme's thumb. If any one resists, he'll be arrested, or killed! The only thing that's saved the President is the fact that when trouble broke he rushed a regiment of Marines here and threw them around the White House. They've been completely loyal to him, but if he's impeached...Besides, the Holme Guard has been busy 'converting' them. Dick, I tell you there's no hope except that eventually the people will learn the truth and there will be a counter-revolution. I really don't think it would do any good to kill Holme."

"That we must not do!" Wentworth said sharply. "Everything depends on his living. I have a plan—"

"It will have to be terribly good, Dick," Nita said. "Holme—my blood runs cold at the thought of him—really believes he's the reincarnation of Abraham Lincoln! These damnable yogis have convinced him of that. Why, he's even growing a beard like Lincoln! Oh, it would be funny if he were not so incredibly powerful."

"His power is our strength," Wentworth said softly. "Then my guesses about the yogis influencing Congressmen—"

"You were right, Dick," Nita said hurriedly. "There must be fully a hundred of those fake yogis in the city and their reputation is amazing. They must have a vast information and investigating service to know so much about so many people."

"Of course!" Wentworth exclaimed, "I'm beginning to understand now how the control over Congress was managed. First, advice from the yogis. Almost anyone will believe such soothsayers, even when they scoff. A corps of investigators like that could get at the secrets of the Congressmen and, where they couldn't influence, they could blackmail! After that came terrorism. By the heavens it must be that Swami Re that Ellen Mayfrew named to me. Or Rass Mehli."

"It's higher, Dick," Nita said fiercely. "It goes much higher than that. Those men are involved, along with countless others, but not even they are at the head of the organization."

"Higher than they?" Wentworth said softly, and his mind flashed back to Ellen Mayfrew and his suspicions of her father. "Now tell me about Yolanda Blanton and her boyfriend, Carl Gresham. They're important to my plan. And about Ellen Mayfrew and Elias Godlove."

Nita stared at him curiously. "How did you know about Ellen and Godlove?" she asked. "He seems to be mad about her."

"I didn't know," Wentworth shook his head. "I didn't mean to couple them. Do you know Yolanda, personally?"

Nita nodded. "I have made a point of it. Carl is there almost every night."

"Then I want you to go to Yolanda's tonight and be there, with Carl and Yolanda, about eleven o'clock. If Carl isn't there, get Yolanda to call him on some pretext."

He brought the car to a halt before the office where Nita worked and for a moment Nita hesitated beside him. "Dick, can't you tell me more! If I only knew how to help you!"

Wentworth's lips softened into a smile. "Darling, you help me just by being! And don't worry. We'll win out."

Wentworth drove steadily back to the room that had been allotted him and threw himself down to rest. Damnable to be weak like this when everything depended on swift, sure action. Damnable to have to deceive Nita with prate of confidence, when their chance was so slim—so slim. If everything worked out just right, and he had gauged Roger Holme accurately, there was an outside chance of success. Otherwise, it must be as Nita said—a long battle against overwhelming odds, a bloody counter-revolution which even at the cost of many lives might fail…And he had no idea of the "man higher up" whom Nita suspected.

It was nine o'clock on the dot when Wentworth presented himself again at the major's office. The major grinned thinly at his promptitude. He laid a much sealed packet of papers on his desk.

"Your job, Blinky," he said softly, "is to burglarize the safe indicated on this drawing of a house and put these papers in it—without being discovered in the act. Understand?"

Blinky McQuade gulped, "And I get five thousand for that?"

"Yes," the major leaned forward impressively. "Yes. You see, the safe you are going to loot is in a bedroom that will be occupied. The bedroom is in the White House. Its occupant will be—the President of the United States!"

CHAPTER TEN
Great Men Can Die

WENTWORTH could scarcely restrain a shout of delight. He would have a chance to see the President, to learn his strength and acquaint him with the plans…But Blinky McQuade must quail in terror. The major reassured him. One of the Marine sentinels would pass him in. Except for the troops, the White House was weakly guarded and a certain window would be unlocked.

Everything fell out precisely as the major had said and within an hour, Wentworth found standing inside a darkened office in the White House. He was bitterly angry at these evidences of treachery within this utmost sanctuary of government, but it had warned him. He must speak to no one but the President, himself.

The floor plan with which he had been provided guided him unfalteringly through dimly lighted corridors and he came at last to a window which, opening on a roof, gave him access to a window of the President's bedchamber. He stepped inside soundlessly, stood at the foot of the bed where the great man slept quietly, arms unflung like a boy's.

"Mr. President," Wentworth called softly. "Mr. President, I have an important message for you."

Before he had finished the sentence, the half-light of the room showed him the gleam of the President's eyes. He saw another gleam, too—a gun in his hand!

The President said dryly, "I have a gun. How in the hell did you get here?"

"I was hired by the Holme Guard," Wentworth told him quietly. "A sentinel betrayed his trust, and someone inside the house left a window open by arrangement. Whom I don't know. Please talk to me alone. I don't know who betrayed you and if he sees me this way, it will cost my life. I am plotting to overthrow Holme."

The President hitched himself higher in the bed, turned on a small bedside lamp and tilted the shade so that its light focused on Wentworth's face. The President was smiling slightly, his big intelligent head lifted.

"That's a major undertaking. May I ask who you are?"

Wentworth smiled back at him, "I am known generally, I believe, as the *Spider*."

For long moments, the two men regarded each other. Presently, the President drew in a long breath and nodded. "If you can prove your identity, and I can help you, I will. Holme's men are guilty of ten thousand crimes. They're robbing the citizens all over the country. My veto is futile to stop the looting of the Treasury. I hope your plan is a good one...Now, your proofs."

Wentworth handed him the packet which was to have been planted in his safe and the President's face suffused with angry blood as he glanced through them. "They didn't need to do a thing like this," he said bitterly. "They're going to impeach me tomorrow. Perhaps tonight! And they won't need such trumped-up evidence as this! This would prove me guilty of looting the Treasury, myself! You've proved you're a friend."

Impassively, Wentworth leaned forward and affixed the seal of the *Spider* to one of the documents.

"Tell me two things only, sir," he said. "Is the Navy loyal? It is? Good! Then I can block this impeachment, so far as legality is concerned. If there is a legal technicality, you can resist being removed from here. Cement the Marines to yourself by personal loyalty. The Holme Guards have been at work on them. And hold the White House against all comers! I know, of course, you have no means of getting in touch with the Navy."

The President smiled faintly, his eye corners crinkling. "How will you prevent a legal impeachment, *Spider*?"

Wentworth's own lips were grim. The vote for impeachment, to be legal, must be by two-thirds of the entire Senate. Not two-thirds of those present, but of the entire Senate.

The President nodded in agreement.

"More than a third of the senators are loyal to you, sir."

"Not a chance of their upholding me," the President said curtly. "A vote for me would be repaid by murder tomorrow. And every one of those men knows it!"

Wentworth leaned forward slightly. "Yes. But if they weren't there to vote? If they were aboard one of the battleships at sea?"

"By the Lord Harry, you're bold, *Spider!*" The President laughed. "Can you kidnap a third of the Senate?"

"I have a plan," Wentworth said curtly. "If you will tell me the whereabouts of the fleet and give me a written order to the commander. Fine! Now, then—the second question. Do you believe that if Holme recanted his power; that if he told the people his men were no better than outlaws, and appealed to the people to overthrow them, the people would obey? The Navy could support that movement by arming civilian armies."

"Are you mad?" the President was leaning forward, some of the laxness of age and despair gone from his face. "Are you completely mad? Holme would never do such a thing!"

Wentworth jerked his head impatiently. "He will. I ask you—would the people be able to conquer? Would the Holme Guard have the morale to continue if they were disowned publicly by Holme?"

Slowly, the President sank back on his pillows. He shook his head wearily. "Granted that these impossible things could be done," he said slowly, "we would win, yes. But there is not a chance in the world that Holme would do such a thing."

Wentworth smiled thinly, "That's the *Spider's* task. Sir, be very careful of yourself and your employees. One at least has betrayed you by that opening of a window. And, to the last man, resist being put out of the White House. Your life would not be worth a cent once the Marines were no longer around you. And America needs you very badly, Mr. President."

Wentworth pivoted toward the window, but the President called him back. "I have been a prisoner in my house since the day Holme struck his first blow over a month ago," he said slowly. "I have been unable to reach my people or the Navy by radio, or any other means. Only a few messages trickle through to me. And I think I was losing hope. I am behind you to the last breath of life, *Spider*. God give you strength and the genius you will need."

Wentworth laughed and took the President's proferred hand. "What I need chiefly is two large transport planes, if I'm going to kidnap thirty-five senators! I have a list of those who can be counted on to oppose Holme. Good night, sir, and God keep you."

He stole from the White House grounds by the same route he had entered, phoned to the major. "This is Blinky," he said. "It was a cinch!"

He was ordered to report in the morning, which suited his plans perfectly. He phoned Nita at Yolanda's home and spoke rapidly in French. "This is the most important part of my entire plan, Nita," he said, "but I cannot do it personally. Another pressing thing has sprung up that must be attended to at once. Have you anyone you can call on for help? Ram Singh is here! Perfect...Now, listen carefully. Take Gresham and Yolanda's son to Hoover Airport an hour from now—without Yolanda. God bless you, Nita. Remember, if this fails; everything fails. If Gresham opposes too violently, recall to him that Yolanda has said she would go with him if she were free. And tell him that this is the path to freedom! Good night, love. Guard yourself!"

WENTWORTH was frowning heavily as he left the cigar-store phone booth. He could depend on Nita's ingenuity, in Ram Singh's strength, but it was a perilous assignment for a woman—this abduction of the lover and child of a woman who was high priestess of the nation and mistress to its master! Then he laughed sardonically. He had given himself a far greater task—and it led first to the home of Ellen Mayfrew—Senator Ellen Mayfrew, for she had been appointed to her father's seat because of her loyalty to the cause that had slain that father!

In the sedan which carried him swiftly to the Mayfrew home, Wentworth made some swift changes in his appearance. Over the grey hair of Blinky McQuade he drew a lank wig of long black hair. The removal of the glasses and certain plates which had made Blinky's lips loose and pendulous completed the change. A black cape drawn about his shoulders, a wide-brimmed hat—and the *Spider* stole from the car to be swallowed by the shadows beneath the trees!

In an intimate small parlor in the Mayfrew mansion, Elias Godlove stood over Ellen where she sat upon a low couch. Her dress was exquisite, heavy black silk that modeled to her slightest movement and left the warm ivory of her shoulders and throat bare. Godlove's eyes roved gloatingly over her. Abruptly, his long hands seized Ellen's shoulders and dragged her up into his embrace. His thin-lipped mouth was open in his eagerness, his voice hoarse and panting.

"You've stalled me long enough!" he cried. "Now, tonight..."

Ellen twisted free, backed slowly away. "You're mad!" she whispered. "You have no right..."

Godlove laughed, wildly. "No right? So you've been fooling me, you witch! But that's over. I should have offered you riches, a throne. Now, you shall be my slave. You dare to defy me—me, Elias Godlove, commander of the faithful! Who's to stop me?"

From the window came a man's laughter, flat, mocking, sinister, "I shall stop you, Godlove...forever!" A black-caped figure, face masked in the shadow of his hat's brim, stepped over the sill. Godlove whirled to face him.

"You!" he cried hoarsely. "Who are you that you dare to enter and challenge me!"

The laughter came again, "I am...the *Spider!*"

With the words, the *Spider* glided toward Godlove. The commander backed slowly, hand fumbling at his holster, furtively. Cursing, he whipped his revolver free and the *Spider* leaped. His left hand clamped on chamber and hammer of Godlove's gun, his right swung an automatic savagely against his head. The blow knocked Godlove from his grip, hurled him sideways to the floor. His head struck against a table leg with a sickening sound. Wentworth turned toward Ellen Mayfrew; traitress or ally of a masquerading father, it did not matter just now.

"Get your cloak," he ordered harshly. "You go with me!"

Ellen was pale to the lips but without fright, "I'll have to...now. With him dead, my life isn't worth a dime. But I'm glad. I'm *glad!* He deserved death a thousand times." Her clenched hands were shaken in the air and she calmed but slowly. "You return to Washington too late, *Spider*. Tonight, the Senate impeaches the President!"

"Tonight!" Wentworth cried.

Ellen nodded. "And they'll call a national election for two days from now to elect Holme President-dictator for fifteen years. The Holme Guard will see that the people elect him!"

Wentworth's mouth twisted as he stared down at the dead man. The woman's words filled him with alarm, but was she sincerely hostile to Holme and his organization? "You were a priestess of Siva," Wentworth said softly. "You're an ally of your father's murderers!"

Ellen held out her clenched white fists. "Do you think that only men love vengeance!" she cried. Her eyes were bleak.

Wentworth frowned. She *sounded* sincere..."Get your cloak. Phone the Senate president that these are Godlove's orders: There shall be no vote on the impeachment until Godlove comes." He laughed harshly. "They'll believe an order from Godlove's woman! Your vengeance has begun!"

IT WAS a half hour later that a man who wore the gold-encrusted uniform of Godlove, who walked with his lean swagger, and spoke with his harsh voice mounted the steps of the Capitol with Ellen Mayfrew beside him. He stopped before two Holme guards at the door who stiffened to salute.

The man snapped orders, "Go to the airport and have two of the largest cabin ships fueled and warmed up." The guard he had addressed saluted and ran to obey. To the other, the man who spoke with Godlove's voice said, "Commandeer a half dozen sedans and summon a motorcycle escort. *Sergeant of the guard!*" A non-commissioned officer came at a run as the second guard started off. "Two squads of men, bayonets, at once. I have some arrests to make."

When the sergeant had gone, Ellen's hand rested briefly on the man's arm.

"If I did not know he was dead," she said softly, "I, myself, would swear you were Godlove."

Wentworth silenced her. "Columns have ears as well as walls. I *am* Godlove. He went striding into the Capitol as the sergeant returned with double-squad of men carrying rifles and fixed bayonets. No one seemed to notice that Wentworth stood in the shadow as he drew out a beribboned paper.

"I have here a warrant for the arrest of thirty-six senators," he said. "Serve it, Sergeant, and take them to the airport. I'll follow. But first of all, say to the Chief that I await him in his office on an imperative matter."

The sergeant saluted, took the paper Wentworth had forged on one of a packet of signed warrants-in-blank which Godlove had carried.

"Remember, Sergeant," Wentworth cautioned. "The message to the Chief first!"

The sergeant smiled faintly. "Understood, Commander!" He marched off with his men, and Wentworth turned to Ellen.

"Now your job begins, Ellen," he said. "Go to his office and say that you prevailed on me to call him. Say that you don't believe the President is guilty and, given time, you will prove it. Appeal to his sense of justice, Ellen."

Ellen's hand closed hard on Wentworth's. "God be with you, *Spider*. My task is easy beside yours." She walked off along the corridor, a regal figure in her long, swirling cape. Her life was at stake, too, if Godlove's body were found too soon...Wentworth strode down the steps, stood waiting beside the official car that had been at Ellen's home. The sergeant presently marched the senators to the cars. Some protested almost tearfully; some were silent and resigned and all were bitterly frightened. But none resisted. They had learned that death came swiftly to those who rebelled against the orders of the guard!

SO FAR things had gone smoothly, almost too smoothly. Wentworth's eyes kept wary watch as he waited. But Ellen would hold Holme. His danger now lay at the airport where bright lights might betray his masquerade. Give him a half hour aloft in the planes and he would defy all the air force to find him. As the last of the senators was herded into the cars, Wentworth sprang into Godlove's.

"The airport—fast!" he ordered raspingly.

Swiftly, in his mind, Wentworth checked the details of his plan and could find no fault with it. If only Nita and Ram Singh were on hand with Gresham and the boy...From a hundred yards away, he made sure that the planes were warming up according to schedule. But his eyes, questing over the airport as they approached, searched in vain for Nita. He sprang from the car, rasped orders which packed the senators into the planes, dismissed all save a few of the guards, sent the commandeered cars speeding back to the city—and still no sign of Nita!

Wentworth glanced anxiously at his watch. It was twenty minutes past the hour he had set for her arrival. His lips grew thin with apprehension, but he could wait no longer. He entered one plane and searched out a senator he knew to be an experienced pilot. He had counted on Ram Singh to handle one of the ships, but now...He hailed the senator to the cockpit, where the pilot sat.

"Check your fuel loads," Wentworth ordered the pilot.

"Already done, sir," the pilot replied.

Wentworth said raspingly, "Must I repeat an order?"

The pilot scrambled out and Wentworth faced the senator, spoke in his normal voice. "There was a plot to kill you all tonight," he said quietly. "We are flying to join the fleet which still is loyal. Can you follow my plane in the air?"

The senator stared wide-eyed, then he frowned. "Who are you?" he demanded harshly.

Wentworth drew out the President's orders to the Navy commander and the senator made no more difficulty. He thrust out his hand.

"We are your debtors, sir," he said. "I'll follow you to hell and back!"

Wentworth nodded. "Keep me in sight. And remember, regardless of who seems to be sending or what the question, answer no radio signals whatever—or our enemies may find us. Knock out that pilot when he returns and tie him up."

Wentworth stepped down from the plane, crossed to the other. Still no sign of Nita! Beneath its disguise, his face was pale and drawn. God! If they had caught her! But he could not delay, could not! The pilot stood by the door of the second plane.

"You are dismissed," Wentworth told him shortly.

The pilot stared, "I didn't know you could fly, Commander," he said hesitantly. "You…why…*you—aren't—Godlove!*" His voice rose to a scream. He spun away from Wentworth, shouting. "This man is an impostor. He's not our commander, Godlove!"

CHAPTER ELEVEN
While Death Waits

IT WOULD have been possible for Wentworth to jump into the plane and take off before anyone could interfere, but pursuit immediately might defeat his plans. He could shoot the man dead—Godlove's acts would not be questioned—but it was not the Spider's habit to kill needlessly. The man had committed no offense save loyalty to his commander.

Wentworth's voice rose tremendously, drowning out the man's shout, soaring even above the idling of the planes' motors.

"Arrest that man!" he cried.

Guards stared at the running man, at Wentworth's sternly pointing arm, then closed in on the pilot. While they ran him down, Wentworth fumbled behind him with a pocket-knife and slightly damaged a control wire. When the guards wrestled the pilot, half unconscious from blows, up to the plane, Wentworth pointed dramatically to the wire.

"Sabotage!" he cried. "Hold the traitor incommunicado until my return. Get me another pilot at once."

When the second pilot reached the cockpit, he found the radio temporarily out of commission. Wentworth brushed that fact aside as of no importance.

"The course is due west," he ordered sharply. "Crowd on all the altitude you can.

The ship lifted smoothly from the field and the second ship took off in its wake. Wentworth settled into the co-pilot's seat. He could restore the radio at a moment's notice. When the time came, he would get the help of some of the younger senators in tying up the pilot after he had slugged him and explain the situation to them. It would be daylight before he was near the position of the fleet. And behind him, at grips with that damnable gang of murderous conspirators, he had left Nita—had abandoned her. And at the very least, it would be twenty-four hours before he could return to the airport…

Actually, it was nearly midnight of the next night—of the eve of the election of Roger Holme as Dictator-President—when Wentworth circled the big empty plane above the landing-field at Washington. He had had a battle all the way through storms from the moment of his almost disastrous take-off from the fleet's plane-carrier. He had been compelled to take on only a barely sufficient supply of gas to give him lightness enough for a take-off on that short run. The captive pilot was bound in the cockpit.

"Remember," Wentworth said curtly. "Open your mouth, and I'll have you shot as a traitor!"

The pilots jaws were set angrily, but he nodded curtly—and Wentworth set the plane smoothly down on the field. He had no way of knowing what awaited him here. Godlove's body might have been found, or the arrested pilot might convince people of the truth. And Holme—even if Wentworth succeeded in maintaining his imposture, what would Holme have to say to the lieutenant who had acted so drastically without consulting him?

A squad of guards formed double ranks beside the door of the plane. Wentworth loosened his revolver in its holster, uncuffed the pilot and motioned him ahead.

"You're going with me," he said shortly.

At the door, Wentworth gravely returned the salute of the sergeant and the guard. The sergeant stepped forward and Wentworth waited coldly. Within seconds now, he would know…

"Commander," the sergeant said briskly. "The chief's orders: Report to him personally immediately on landing."

Wentworth saluted, scarcely squeezing the smile off his lips. His heart leaped exultantly. His imposture had not been discovered then! This fitted perfectly with his plans…

"Sergeant, accompany me," he ordered. "You, also." He nodded at the pilot. Moments later, a sedan preceded by siren-shrieking motorcycles sped him toward the city. "Our radio went bad," Wentworth told the sergeant. "Any news of importance?"

"Plenty, Commander!" The sergeant spun out rapidly the fact that the rump senate had voted to impeach the President, but that, supported by his Marines, the President refused to leave the White House and claimed the impeachment was illegal. Wentworth lowered his eyes to hide the satisfaction in them, saw startled intelligence leap into the face of the pilot who spun toward him furiously. Wentworth laid his hand upon his holster and the man subsided. Fight had left him.

"And there's been a kidnapping, sir," the sergeant ran on. "Mrs. Blanton's boy and a young fellow named Gresham were snatched just before you took off. No clue to who did it, but Mrs. Blanton is almost crazy, they say. We'll win the election tomorrow, of course."

Wentworth's lips set grimly. "Of course!" Yes, it was sure as that unless he accomplished what the President of the United States and everyone else would call impossible. Let the people once confirm Holme in his office and the little pretense of legality that was maintained would be thrown off. The Holme Guard would openly loot and destroy, terrorize the entire country. But Wentworth was going to do the impossible, or die in the attempt! If only he knew where Nita was...

AT HOLME'S residence, the doors were instantly flung wide and Wentworth stalked in, bidding the sergeant good-by with thanks. As Wentworth entered the room where Holme waited, alone, he snaked his revolver from its holster and struck the pilot hard across the skull. Holme sprang to his feet and Wentworth faced him across the width of a sumptuous office.

"What is the meaning of this?" Holme demanded curtly. "You wrecked the impeachment proceedings by abducting those senators! Come, talk fast. You've a great deal of explaining to do!"

Wentworth eyed the senator calmly. It was the first time he had seen the man since nearly two months before. A young beard was beginning to shape into a likeness of the famous Lincoln beard and there was the same hard-boned gauntness of frame here, the funereal garb. But the lift of the head was too challenging and neither kindliness, nor humbleness of spirit was in his eyes. Wentworth went deliberately toward him, gun still in hand. He was watching him like a hawk.

"Put up your hands!" he ordered curtly, "and come out from behind that desk!"

Holme's eyes tightened. Wentworth had spoken in his normal tone of voice, but with a steady force that told of confidence and ample strength. Holme, nevertheless, did not obey. He leaned forward, placing both hands on the desk.

"Godlove never spoke like that," he said softly. "You...You are not Godlove! An assassin?" Holme laughed. "I do not fear assassins! I was killed once by a murderer's bullet in a previous life. That is not to be my fate again!"

Those damnable yogis and their lies!

Wentworth reached Holme's side in a lithe stride and with a swinging wrench whirled him from behind the desk. Holme shut his lips angrily, clenched his fists...

Wentworth leveled the gun, "Stay there, Holme. Much as I admire your foolhardy courage, it will not keep me from killing you if necessary. Haven't you recognized me yet, Holme? I am the *Spider!*"

Holme stiffened, swung toward the door. His intention to summon the guard was plain enough. With an exasperated curse, Wentworth leaped. He swung the gun lightly, but it hammered Holme unconscious to the floor.

With deft movements then, Wentworth strapped his arms to his sides, put a light gag in his lips and quickly revived him. When Holme's eyes opened, Wentworth began to talk swiftly.

"Holme, you have been betrayed," he said. "That is the reason you are alive today. I have been convinced from the first that you were the victim of the people who pretend to help you. I believe you are a just man. Will you promise to listen to me for ten minutes without interruption? If, at the end of that time, you do not believe me, I will surrender to your mercy!" His eyes shone with truth.

Holme nodded slowly, his eyes deeply intent on Wentworth's face. "Ten minutes," he said shortly, when Wentworth removed the gag.

With quick words then, Wentworth told the entire story of his personal battle against the Holme machine, of being hired as Blinky McQuade.

"They sent me to plant certain papers in the safe in the President's private room," he said. "Instead, I have given those papers to the President to be destroyed."

Holme's eyes tightened. "I do not see how you could know about that," he said slowly. "It is true my men reported to me such papers were in existence. I went to the President and failed to find them, but I went privately. Somehow, I find it hard to believe in his guilt."

Wentworth said softly: "You did that because you are fundamentally a just man. You were unwilling for the President to be deposed if he were innocent." He hurried on without giving him time to reply, telling about the major who once had headed a white-slavery racket, of the gunman who had deliberately shot down Daniel Borough—and been killed by his friends—of the evil cult that worshipped Siva.

"Let me prove these facts to you," Wentworth said softly. "Listen, Yolanda, herself, is a victim of these same men. She will tell you so when we go to her."

Holme's head snapped up. "I do not believe that!" he said harshly. "No woman could have foretold the things she has, and not be truly gifted with the second sight!"

Wentworth smiled. "Unless the things that she forecast had been preordained by the gang! And she informed of facts! The attempt on your life in which you were not hurt? That was a planned assassination of Daniel Borough! The facts you disclosed about grafters? The result of clever detective work by Godlove and his men. Your own victories? Your very confidence in success helped to establish those—and the crooked work of Godlove and his men!"

Holme shook his head stubbornly. "It is impossible. I do not believe you!"

Wentworth slowly freed Holme's hands. "You are too just to say that you do not believe, if you really do," he said quietly. "I am ready to surrender."

Holme strode toward the door but his step slowed. He turned to face Wentworth. "I do not believe," he said heavily, "but I cannot deny you have raised doubts. If only you could offer proof..."

"I can offer proofs," Wentworth said shortly. "Come with me. But here is a proof of my own belief. The *Spider* has never tried to kill you!"

Holme stared without comprehension, and Wentworth continued softly, "The *Spider* boasts that he never yet has killed an innocent man. Yet, if I considered you guilty of the infamies that have been perpetrated in your name, you would have died weeks ago!"

Holme shrugged impatiently, "You offered proofs."

Wentworth nodded. "Order that pilot held incommunicado until we return, and come with me."

Holme nodded slowly and agreed. A few minutes later, alone in a powerful coupe, they sped together across the city. "Would it help convince you," Wentworth asked, "if I proved that there are over a half hundred criminals on the payrolls of the Holme Guard at tremendous salaries? We can get fingerprint men from the Department of Justice, go to the barracks and get the records of pay."

Holme moved a hand impatiently. "Perhaps."

AT THE Department of Justice, Holme strode directly to the office of the director. "Perhaps this will be a short-cut." he said curtly. "I have every confidence in this man."

The director stared at him coldly as Holme

stalked into his office. Holme asked a single direct question, and a slight smile stirred the director's lips.

"Do you want a truthful answer or whitewash?" he asked curtly.

Holme frowned and his voice became thunderous. "I am called the Sword of Justice and I am just! This man says there are famous criminals on the rolls here. This man is…not Godlove as he seems."

The director's eyes swept briefly over Wentworth's face. He nodded. "The disguise is very clever, however. If you want the truth—you have been correctly informed. I can give you a full list of the criminals. Frankly, Senator, I was informed they were hired at your express orders—by Godlove."

Holme's face drew into harsh lines and cold fire began to burn in his eyes. "Thanks," he said curtly, and wheeled to leave.

"A moment, Holme," Wentworth said quietly. "Mr. Director, at a certain address in the Southeast district, on the night of September the eighth, there was a fire. I think it very likely your men were called there."

The director nodded quietly, "Godlove said it was quite all right," he said. "Against Godlove and his men I was—am—powerless, but I kept the records for a reckoning."

Holme said, his voice muffled in anger, "What did you find there—if anything?"

"A mechanical idol some thirty feet high," the director said shortly. "There were many bodies in the ruins. The body in the hands of the idol was identified as that of Supreme Court Justice McTavish."

In a strangled voice, Holme demanded, "Where is Godlove?"

The director looked at Wentworth and shrugged slightly. "It is my guess that Godlove has paid for some of his crimes," he said quietly. Holme stared at Wentworth, also, started to speak, then closed his lips harshly.

"I am ready for further proofs," he said finally.

Wentworth left with Holme and soon they were in the car again. Wentworth began to talk swiftly, "You were kept in ignorance of these things, but they were all done in your name. Throughout the country, a thousand crimes are being daily committed in your name. But I tell you, Godlove is not responsible alone. There is some one behind him, some one I do not know. This some one has directed the yogis who had given you false information as 'revelations'. He is profiting by this wholesale crime. He will see that you are elected tomorrow and made Dictator-President of the nation. If necessary, he will imprison you then and rule in your stead."

Holme's head swayed. "I cannot believe it." he said dully. "I…I *am* the reincarnation of Lincoln! I am *just!* I have wiped out corruptions…"

"A great deal of it," Wentworth agreed quietly, "but there is a large class of people to whom power is useful only for personal gain. They have risen in your shadow. They have kept you in ignorance…"

"But the newspapers!" Holme cried. "The radio! If the people were tricked like that, they would cry out through those media!"

Wentworth's smile was thin and twisted. "You own every radio station, every newspaper in the country, Holme," he said. "They have been seized in your name."

Holme's head slowly came up. "It is impossible," he said flatly. "It could not be."

"Will you believe…Yolanda?" Wentworth asked quietly. "If she tells you that her inspirations have been human; that she has told you nothing but lies through the months; that she, too, is a slave of the power that fattens on your work—will you believe?"

Holme groaned and dropped his head into his hands. "As God is my witness, I do not know. I'm afraid that if Yolanda tells me that…But why, why would she deceive me?"

Wentworth told him swiftly then of the threat held over her son as the price of obedience, the torture of her son. He was racing for Yolanda's home now. "You and you alone can straighten out this conspiracy," Wentworth said softly. "If you swing your support to the President, you will wipe out the criminals who have used your name as a cover for infamy.

You will prove yourself really a Sword Of Justice! A radio speech by yourself—broadcast throughout the nation during the morning voting hours—throwing your support to the President..."

"The President is a grafter!"

Wentworth shook his head. "The President has been framed as have many other men. Many of the senators who support you have been blackmailed into it. I swear this to you, Holme. I, the *Spider*, who have never sworn to a falsehood!"

Holme beat his temples with his fists. "Yolanda," he whispered. "If she says you speak the truth..."

WENTWORTH jerked the coupe to a halt. They were before Yolanda's home, which blazed with lights. His heart beat high and strongly in his breast. He was winning. By the heavens, he was winning—accomplishing the impossible! Yolanda would talk when she learned that he and not the men of the Holme Guard, of the Cobra, had kidnapped her son; that he was safe from torture. And then would come...

On the pavement, Wentworth stopped in his tracks, staring at the brilliantly lighted house. Within was no sound, no movement. A shout rose in his throat. With Holme at his heels, he dashed across the pavement. The front door swung open beneath the pressure of his hand. He darted inside.

"Yolanda!" Wentworth shouted. *"Yolanda!"*

Holme echoed his cry and the silence of the house, their own emptily echoing voices beat back upon them. They dashed up the stairs and in the hallway lay a dead man, a Hindu on whose forehead burned the symbol of the Cobra. All about them was death, and the traces of death. Four other men were sprawled before the doorway of Yolanda's small upstairs parlor. But the door was splintered! Wentworth sprang into the room.

Empty! Empty save for one man sprawled upon the floor, a man who stirred feebly as Wentworth bent over him. Good God. Ram Singh! Then, Nita, too...

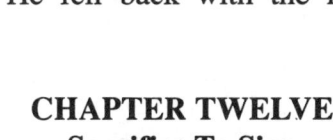

"The Cobra!" Ram Singh whispered. "The men of the Cobra...The woman and...the *missie sahib*..." His eyes closed and he sagged back. His breath came in great gasped groans, but presently words came, too. *"Missie sahib* say...*Cave mortuum qui vivit!'"*

Wentworth cried out violently, "She said...*what?*" Anxiously, he hunted out whiskey and dribbled some down Ram Singh's throat. Wentworth's face was taut and abruptly haggard. Nita had been here and had been seized, too, by the men of the cobra and she had left a clue, a cabalistic clue. She must not have known until the men had crashed into the room. She...God! Death and defeat in the moment of victory!

Ram Singh's eyes opened a narrow way, and his lips fumbled out the same halting phrase. He fell back with the limpness of death!

CHAPTER TWELVE
Sacrifice To Siva

WENTWORTH sprang to his feet, reached a telephone in a long stride and curtly ordered an ambulance. He knelt tenderly beside the Sikh and his eyes were grim at sight of the gashed wound in his side. He had lost a great deal of blood...Against the wall, Holme stood like a man bereft of life. He roused presently and stumbled toward Wentworth.

"What has happened here?" he demanded.

Wentworth swore. "The men who use your

name got to Yolanda first," he said savagely. "The same bunch that killed Justice McTavish by giving him to a mechanical idol to tear to bits with its hands!"

Holme shook his head heavily. "We must find her," he said. "Find her quickly. She can tell me the truth."

"If she lives long enough!" Wentworth hurled at him. "We were left a clue with this Sikh, if we can read it."

"You mean what he said," Holme was swaying on his feet. "It sounded like Latin to me. *Cave*—Beware."

Wentworth sprang to his feet, the phrase suddenly taking meaning in his brain. Nita had not known sufficient Hindustani to use. There must have been a reason for not employing French. Latin! *Cave mortuum qui vivit!* He

"The Cobra," Ram Singh whispered. "The men of the Cobra! The woman and the *missie sahib* ..."

repeated the phrase out loud and his eyes stared blankly into the eyes of Senator Holme.

"Beware the dead who walks!"

Holme said angrily, "It doesn't mean anything. The Hindu got it wrong. What dead? How can dead people walk?"

Wentworth did not answer. He was staring at the wall and a cry burst from his lips. *"The dead who lives"* But it could be any of the many who had "died." Daniel Borough. Senator Mayfrew. And yet Ellen had seemed to help. By the heavens…

Holme nodded, his eyes keen on Wentworth's face. "The phrase means something to you?"

"Perhaps," Wentworth told him. "I do not know. It seems incredible...God, if that ambulance would only come!"

It came soon and Wentworth pressed money on the intern. "Save that man's life at all costs," he said violently. "He needs a transfusion immediately. His blood type is AO. Confirm it if you must, but get the right kind of donor at the hospital at once. Test it after you get there." He stood for a moment beside the panting, unconscious Ram Singh, then spun to Holme, "Come, if you still need proof," he said harshly.

IT WAS a drive of fifteen blocks and at the end of the trail was a tightly boarded mansion. Wentworth raced, soft-footed, for its side and forced open a basement window, leaped in first with Holme fumbling after him. Wentworth lacked a torch, but a match showed him an empty, cement-floored basement. He shook his head, ran for the steps upward. He had to be right. He was right—or Nita died! And Yolanda died—and with them both died all hope of saving the country on the morrow.

The first floor of the house was shrouded in dust; ghostly covers lay over the furniture. "This place is familiar," Holme whispered.

Wentworth struck a match, started up stairs to the second floor and paused, pointing. Glistening there was a drop of blood! Wentworth's eyes probed into the darkness above stairs, but there was no movement, no sound. Gun in hand, he stole upward with Holme at his heels. Wentworth felt a sharp impatience at the man. If he could use the gun, he might be useful, but few could move as soundlessly as the *Spider*. To his sensitive ears, Holme's advance was like a cavalry charge.

On the second floor, Wentworth paused only a few moments. There could be no room here large enough for—for the needs of the Hindus. His eyes lifted to the ceiling above and faintly the sound of moving feet came to his ears, dimly a chanting like that he remembered terribly. In a frenzy, he hunted for stairs that led upward—and found none.

Finally, he discovered another thing, pointed out by the trail of glittering blood drops—a trapdoor that led upward. There was no ladder, but a chair upon a chest gave him a platform by which to mount. He paused for a moment then, ran swiftly to a light-switch. Its click accomplished nothing. Secret cables then must supply the temple beneath the roof, the sound-proofed temple he did not need to see to describe—and dedicated to the worship of Siva the Terrible!

Wentworth sprang to the chair, drew Holme to the top of the chest.

"When I open the trapdoor and jump through," he said swiftly, "you lie low for a moment, then follow. Go to the nearest light and short-circuit the electrical current. Here's a knife to cut the wires. That's the only thing that will stop the torture machine. Let nothing on earth stop you!"

Without another word, Wentworth began to inch the trapdoor upward. He was staring squarely into the malignant face of a squat and awful Siva—and in its torturing hands was...*the lovely white body of a woman!*

Violently, Wentworth threw the trap-door open and hurled himself upward. Once more, he saw the lines of yellow-robed priests, the Hindu torturers, and his gun leaped in his hand, filled the low attic room with thunder. Men were hurled backward to bloody death or pitched writhing to the floor. Seconds passed. Knives flashed through the air toward him, and he dodged. The yellow-robed priests were massing to attack—and still the dim lights burned, still those powerful hands twisted the beautiful limbs of its victims. Her screams rang out terribly.

The hammer of Wentworth's single gun clicked on an empty chamber and he dared a glance toward the trapdoor. It was closed and over it crouched a Hindu, naked to the waist, who was wiping from the blade of his knife an ominous red stain. Wentworth cursed violently. His eyes flung about in a quest for Holme, but it was plain that he had been stabbed and tossed back below. With a shout, Wentworth sprang to meet the charging priests, dodged aside when the men were almost upon him and sprinted for the nearest light. A knife burned through the flesh of his side, scraped against his ribs. Wentworth laughed wildly as he tore it out.

"Thanks, fools!" he shouted.

WITH a slash of the knife, he cut through the electric wires. The shock of it hurled him ten feet, but darkness slapped instantly down on the room. And he knew the awful mechanical torture of that idol was halted. The shock had dazed Wentworth. He dragged himself limply along the floor toward a far corner of the temple. Shouts were all about him, curses and screams of fear. Shoulders against the wall, Wentworth methodically thumbed fresh cartridges into the revolver. Over near the middle of the room, a muffled gun began to thunder, but he could see no flame. The realization of truth came to him slowly: Holme firing upward through the trapdoor.

His gun reloaded, Wentworth managed to push himself to his feet. He ground a palm against the knife slash in his side. It didn't seem serious, but his strength was debilitated by his long illness. It wouldn't take much to put him out. Wild laughter pumped to Wentworth's lips. The hell it wouldn't! Nothing short of death would stop him!

He bumped against the idol before he was aware he was near, crawled upon the altar and reached upward with his gun hand. His knuckles touched flesh, but it was unresponsive. Had she fainted, or…With a shudder he could not repress, Wentworth remembered the manner of Justice McTavish's death, his neck wrung like a fowl's. Cumbersomely, he mounted on the knees of the idol, fumbled with the fingers of one of the hands that gripped the girl's wrist. Yolanda or Nita? He had been unable to tell in the dim lightning of the room.

"Nita?" he whispered, and the sound was almost a sob, as he fought that stubborn mechanical hand. It yielded finally. An eternity passed while he struggled with those gripping hands. Almost fearfully, he groped for a pulse and found the girl still lived. After that, his movements became frantic. The temple was still filled with fight noise, and that tireless gun still blasted from below.

When the prisoner's weight sagged into Wentworth's arms, he staggered and almost fell. Then he made a heavy way behind the idol, stretched out on his stomach and pointed his gun at darkness, squeezed the trigger. The flash of powder-flame showed him a room empty save for himself and a few scattered bodies of the dead, but in a far corner of the attic temple, another trapdoor made a gaping hole. With a hoarse shout, Wentworth flung to his feet and raced to the aperture by which he had entered.

"Holme!" he shouted. "Holme, they'll be coming in behind you! Watch yourself! I'm coming down through this door!"

Holme's voice rolled up deeply, "Right you are!"

Wentworth gasped with relief, tugged open the trapdoor. When the Hindus tried to crash the room below, they were met by a cross-fire from above and from one side which quickly glutted then with battle. They fled screaming and Wentworth staggered wearily to his feet, pushed heavily toward the idol and struck a match.

The woman behind the idol screamed despairingly. "If you come a step nearer," she stammered, "I'll…I'll kill myself, Elias Godlove!"

Wentworth's shoulders sagged. Not Nita. That was a voice he had come to hate, the voice of Yolanda Blanton. His teeth set on his lip. Holme scrambled up through the trapdoor, came toward them. From somewhere he had found a candle which sent its flickering faint glow before him as he walked.

"Yolanda!" he called eagerly. "Yolanda…"

The woman, hidden behind the idol, sobbed. "Wait a minute, Roger," she cried. "Wait!" She came out presently, wrapped in the yellow robe of a priest. She stared from Holme to Wentworth, frowned.

"You're not…Godlove," she said.

Holme strode toward her anxiously. "Yolanda!" he cried. "You must tell me the truth. Am I truly great? Am I the reincarnation of Lincoln, or is it all trickery as the *Spider* says."

"The *Spider!*" Yolanda shuddered, but when she spoke her voice was wooden. "You are truly great, Roger. You are the spirit of Lincoln."

Wentworth sighed, lifted his head. So much of his strength was wasted and the fight was only begun. And Nita...God in Heaven protect her now!

He said quietly, "Yolanda, your son and Gresham are safe. They were not kidnapped by the men of the Cobra, but by my agents so that you would be free to tell the truth."

Yolanda cried out incoherently. She staggered toward Wentworth. "You lie!" she cried. "You must be lying. No one could...could defeat them!"

Wentworth smiled slightly. The candlelight made the impression ghostly. "If they have your son," he said quietly, "why did they seize and kidnap you? Yolanda, if you confess your trickery now, your son and Gresham will be restored to you safely. If you lie, the enemy will overwhelm us and it will not matter to you what happens afterward. Holme's men will be out to kill him now. Come, speak up. Tell the truth as you told it to me once before, that you told these lies to Holme because if you spoke the truth, they would torture your son to death!"

Yolanda faltered, pressed a hand to her forehead.

"The truth, Yolanda!" Holme thundered.

Yolanda let her hands drop. "It is true, what the *Spider* says," she answered. "None of what I told you was true. I said what I was told to because I had to, or Junior would be tortured. Oh, you cannot blame me..."

Holme stared at her, his fists knotted at his sides. "Blame you?" His voice was empty of feeling. It faltered. "Then, I am not...I am not the spirit of Lincoln?" His voice was pleading now.

Yolanda laughed shortly. "I don't know how you ever swallowed that crap, Roger. I've been primed with what to tell you long before we ever left Indianois."

Holme took a slow step toward her, "But everything you told me for months came true," he said hoarsely. "Everything!"

"Sure," Yolanda agreed. "I never told you anything that the gang hadn't arranged to happen."

Wentworth seized Holme's arm. "You will help now," he said quickly. "You will make that appeal over the radio. Ask your adherents to support the President. It will be the bravest deed of your lifetime! It will make you famous through out the ages."

HOLME stared at Wentworth vacantly; his voice came out as emptily as a child's. "I...I'm afraid," he whispered. "I'm...nothing. Just...Roger Holme. There's no..." He bowed his face in his hands and his shoulders jerked. Hoarse sobs pushed out through his palms.

Incredulously, Wentworth stared at the broken man. How in the name of Heaven had he ever done the things for which he was known! But Wentworth understood. Religion had born out of men's need to lean on something other than themselves. All this man's faith had been pinned on a firm belief that a great man lived again in him. And now he knew that for trickery...A single low oath pushed out of Wentworth's lips. This man could never sway the country by radio! God, in conquering, he had defeated himself. Holme would be elected overwhelmingly through intimidation at the polls, and the man who was behind him would rule him more easily than ever before! It was worse now this way!

Wentworth whirled on Yolanda. "The man from whom you took orders?" he demanded harshly. "Who and where is he?"

The woman shook her head dumbly. "I never saw him," she whispered. "The Hindus brought the messages, made the threats."

Savagely, Wentworth flung from them, ran for the trapdoor. One hope now. He must reach the President, get him on the air somehow...He froze in mid-stride, hearing the slam and chatter of gunfire distantly through the night. He twisted about toward the two.

"Do you know," he demanded hoarsely, "what that is?" Oh, but he knew! He knew even before the words came stumblingly from Yolanda's lips. The Master behind this murder-machine had read his plans before him. He was doing the one thing needed now to make him absolute master of the richest land in the world, to open its coffers to his filching hands, to make him all-powerful.

Yolanda said slowly, "Why, yes, I know. They are going to take the White House by storm and lynch the President."

CHAPTER TWELVE
A Desperate Chance

WENTWORTH stared at Yolanda, incredulity clashing with horror. He strode back toward Holme whose face was ghastly in the wan candlelight. He had clamped his hand on his knife-slashed left arm, but he seemed not to hear the words.

"Did you hear her?" Wentworth demanded roughly. "She says your men are going to lynch the President!"

Holme's head came up slowly. "It's horrible, horrible." He shuddered.

"You can stop them!" Wentworth urged. "Just show yourself, and order them to halt. It's all you have to do!"

Holme's shuddering increased, and Wentworth whirled impatiently away. Perhaps he could once more succeed in mimicking Godlove? He could try, but by the heavens, Holme should go with him!

"You're coming with me," Wentworth ordered shortly, and Holme stumbled forward. Yolanda ran after him.

"What about me?" she cried. "Where is my son?"

Wentworth grinned wolfishly, "Where is the girl who was with you at your house?"

Yolanda shrugged. "Dead, I suppose. You mean...*She* stole Junior?"

Wentworth seized the woman's shoulder, his face gone white. "What do you mean she's dead?" he demanded violently. Yolanda flinched from the fury in his eyes, stammered,

"They didn't bring her here to torture. She was in another car."

Shaken with relief, Wentworth released her. She had no real reason for believing Nita dead, he assured himself—but a captive of the Master she certainly was. Lord, he could not delay here! There was every reason to think the Hindus would return to the attack or summon the Holme Guard. He must speed to the White House and attempt to forestall the murder there. He might succeed if the Master, himself, was not there; if his imposture remained undetected...

At a lurching run, Wentworth burst from the house with Holme in tow, the woman tagging after. A squad of guards was coming toward them at a jog-trot, a half block away. Their guns glinted under a street light. At sight of the three, half glimpsed as they dashed from the house, the guardsmen deployed and threw up their rifles. Wentworth sent Holme and the girl into the coupe.

"Halt!" Wentworth's voice rang out in Godlove's harsh accents. "Halt, you fools! I am your commander!"

"You're the murderer who killed him!" they roared back. "Surrender, or we fire!"

Wentworth threw himself to the ground, as the rifles spoke. He rolled from the curb to the street, sprang to the door of the coupe. He snapped one shot and saw the sergeant go down, wounded in the leg, then Wentworth leaped to the wheel, and hurled the dark coupe down the street. Those rifles were deadly weapons against a car if the men were experienced in their use—and could get the range quickly in this darkness. A bullet would puncture the metal and upholstery, easily.

THE SPIDER fought to keep trees interposed between himself and the rifles, hurtled around the corner with oaths bitter on his lips. The hope of deceiving the troops at the White House was gone!

But there must be a way—there had to be a way to save the President! He was the last hope of snatching the country from absolute tyranny at the hands of criminals. Frantically,

Wentworth sought a course of action while he put distance between himself and the guard. Slowly, a desperate plan began to take form in his mind. Mouth set harshly, he glanced briefly sideways at Holme's face. His head sagged. There was no strength left in him.

If Wentworth failed in his attempt and the election went through, he must keep Holme a prisoner and use him for bait to draw the Master. If the election went through? Wentworth realized that the east was beginning to pale with the sun, that already balloting would be ready to start in some states. And it would be at best an hour before he could put his plan into operation, if at all.

The night-lights of the airport showed dimly ahead, and Wentworth slowed to a normal speed.

"Holme...*Holme!*" he said. "I remember seeing an autogiro at the field two days ago. Do you remember where it's kept?"

Holme shook his head woodenly. Yolanda said promptly, "The middle hangar. What do you want with it? It isn't fast enough for a getaway."

Wentworth turned to Holme. "Do you think you could hold your head up the way you used to—for two minutes?"

Deliberately, he put biting scorn into his voice, but it did not seem to reach Holme.

The senator said dully, "I'll try."

Wentworth was stripping the gold ornaments of command from Godlove's uniform, breaking down the facial disguise in part. He drove straight to the middle hangar.

"Hop out, Holme," he whispered, "and hold your head up!"

Wentworth ran toward the hangar, "The autogiro for the Chief!" he shouted excitedly. A mechanic tumbled from a chair by the door and ran inside, echoing the cry. Men began to bustle about and from the administration building two men in flying-helmets came at a run. Wentworth loosened his revolver in its holster, labored with the men who were rolling the 'giro from the hangar. Holme's head, Wentworth saw, was up, but in pitiful parody of its former challenging strength.

As soon as the ship was clear, one of the mechs sprang to the seat and the self-starter began to whine. Abruptly, the motor burst into a roar of ragged sound. Wentworth strode toward Holme, for whom the men in flying-helmets — pilots, plainly — were heading. Wentworth intercepted them.

"The Chief cannot be disturbed," he said shortly.

The pilots glared at him angrily. "We only want to volunteer as his pilot," one said shortly, then his eye's tightened. "By the devil, I know you. You're..."

Wentworth whipped out his revolver. "Shut your mouth," he ordered grimly. "One more word and you die! Back behind the auto. About face, march!"

He dared not strike the men down. There were too many observers, both in the administration building undoubtedly, and about the 'giro. He would have to hold them here until the motor was completely warmed, then run for it. He knew that within minutes after he took off, machine-gun-armed planes would take the air in pursuit. Yet he could not take the two pilots with him. The maximum capacity of the ship was four passengers; Holme and Yolanda must go.

"Get inside the car," Wentworth ordered curtly.

Sullenly, the men obeyed. With a quick glance at the hangar, Wentworth decided to chance an attack. He slugged the second pilot with the gun as he climbed in, reached for the second, but the man spilled from the car and ran shouting toward the hangar. There was no help for it. Wentworth lined his sights on the man's thigh and fired, bowled him over.

He ran after him, passed Yolanda, "Get Holme into the ship," he ordered curtly. As he ran up to the pilot, he waved the gun wildly over his head. "Damn you!" he shouted. "Talking treason against the Chief! Why should the Chief run away? What has he to run from? Can't the Chief and his girl friend skip out for a few hours without you talking scandal!"

The man had fainted or hit his head in

falling. The mechanics shrank back from Wentworth's wild gun gestures, but one of them grinned and winked. "We'll take care of him," the man said. "You tell the Chief we know how it is. Can't ever have a minute to himself."

Wentworth spun and saw that Holme and Yolanda were inside the ship; the mechanic who had warmed it up was stepping down. But men were running from the administration building. In three long strides, Wentworth was beside the ship and springing to the controls. He yanked the throttle and the motor picked up warmly. He threw the lever which started the overhead rotors spinning. They picked up speed with damnable slowness, flopping like a woman's summer hat. He kept the brakes on the wheels, waiting with an eye on the gauge. The men from the administration building were half the distance to the ship now; some of the mechanics were staring at him with distrust.

WITH a gusty sigh of relief, Wentworth saw the gauge needle swing over, threw the motor power into the propeller. The 'giro jumped twenty-five feet straight upward and calmly windmilled above the heads of the crew below. The western sky was still dark and, lights out Wentworth headed straight into it. He did not need to look back to know what was happening, but no one save a fool would take off in a cold-motored plane. It would take between five and ten minutes to warm one up completely.

Wentworth's lips shut grimly. There might very well be that kind of fools behind him, and they might be lucky enough to be able to hold a cold-motored plane in the air. Resolutely, he swung back over the water, over the park toward the White House. Below him, he could spot the flickering blaze of machine guns from attackers encircling the building. There were two marine emplacements on the roof which blasted out intermittently.

He would have to make his descent quickly. Both sides would take him for an enemy...He searched about him swiftly and found a flashlight, leveled it at the roof and began winking out Morse code signals.

Help for President, he spelled out. *Help for President. Cover us if you can. Don't fire.*

In doing that, he was exposing himself to fire from the Holme Guard, but while the Marines were compelled to be able to read such signals, there was a big chance that the irregulars were not.

Swiftly, then, Wentworth sped toward the White House. There was one flat space he could certainly land on safely in this dead air if he had time to maneuver, but with machine-gun bullets whipping at him from all sides...

Halfway across the length of lawn that slanted up to the south portico of the White House, a machine gun was pointed straight upward and began to spray the air with bullets. Wentworth felt the jar of them ripping up through the fuselage, saw a sliver of torn white on a rotor, but the motor did not falter and no one in the cabin cried out. Wentworth sent the ship down for the roof in a sharp glide, cut the motor and hung by the swirling overhead sails. This was the moment he had dreaded, the moment when, almost stationary, he would make a perfect target for the machine guns a few hundred feet away, outlined against the eastern sky.

"Down on the floor," he ordered shortly. The sides would give no protection, but at least they would have no definite target.

Bullet holes strung across the glass side panels, clattered against the roof, sang off the metal uprights. The wheels jounced heavily on the roof and Wentworth slammed on the brakes. Even so, because of the angle of descent, the ship trundled along until it teetered on the edge of pitching to the earth below. It stopped then and Wentworth kicked open the door, spilled flat to the roof, dragging Holme with him. He found himself staring into the rifles of a squad of Marines, lying flat on the roof, also.

"That was a sweet landing," said the sergeant curtly. "Now who the hell are you?"

"Senator Roger Holme, a prisoner," Wentworth said shortly. "Get us under cover, then you can take word to the President that the man who called to rob his safe one night has come back."

The sergeant's mouth closed like a steel trap. "That's a hell of a message..."

Wentworth's voice snapped in command, "Execute your orders, Sergeant."

The man glared uncertainly for a moment, then jerked his head. "There's a scuttle yonder. Crawl to it."

THE maneuver took minutes. Wentworth heard bullets slam and rattle through the autogiro, and his face drew into grim lines. Not a chance in the world of getting it off again with the President as he had hoped to do—if the motor would even start after that bombardment. Once on the floor below and upright, Wentworth jerked out an order.

"Get the motor started in that 'giro, with the brakes on the wheels, and keep it ticking," he told the sergeant. "If no one up there understands planes, get some one who does. Take me to your superior at once."

The sergeant saluted hesitantly and led the way—but men with ready rifles fell in behind. When Wentworth's curious message went through, he was ushered at once into the President's presence, taking Holme with him.

"I'd like an audience alone, sir," Wentworth said quietly.

The President smiled slowly, jerked his head at the men with him, spoke peremptorily when they dallied.

"Now then, *Spider*," he said. "I heard how you came in."

Wentworth nodded. "I'd hoped to take you out the same way, sir, but it can't be done. They're riddling the plane now. They'll have the range too accurately, even if the ship will still fly. You knew my plan."

The President's shrewd, kindly eyes went to Holme, remained there. "I haven't seen you, Mr. Holme," he said quietly, "since you came to find the evidence in my safe."

Holme lifted his head. "I'm sorry, sir," he mumbled.

The President's eyes narrowed a little. He looked quickly to Wentworth. "Holme knows now," Wentworth said quietly, "that he has been victimized by the men he put in power. He knows that this woman who gave him 'messages' was a fake. But I'm afraid his appeal over the radio would be valueless. There is only one hope. You must speak yourself."

The President said quietly, "Very well. How will you arrange it?" He smiled. It was very wonderful to Wentworth that this man could still smile in the face of this storming of his citadel, in the face of the almost certain death ahead. It was the face of a fighter, the lift of genuine courage. It would take more than the knowledge that he had been deceived to destroy this man's faith.

Wentworth could not resist smiling back, "You are very calm about it, sir."

The President's smile widened, "You've already done several impossible things. If you say you can arrange the radio facilities, I'll believe."

Wentworth sobered. "It isn't simple as that. Our one hope is Arlington. We'll have to crush out of here, and it will cost lives."

"Yes," the President agreed somberly. "But if we stay here, these poor loyal men win die, anyway. I have offered to surrender twice. They know that if we lose this battle, we lose the nation, too. What is your plan?"

"It will have to be fast," Wentworth said. "Are you sure of everyone in the building?"

The President shook his head sadly, "No. But General Foulard can be trusted absolutely. We need tell no one else our full plan." He sent for the general and Wentworth swiftly unfolded his plan. An attack down the south slope; a crush-out with three or four automobiles mounting machine guns at the north into Pennsylvania Avenue, the last timed to follow the south attack and the attempt to lift the 'giro from the roof.

"I'll volunteer for that last job," Wentworth said quietly.

General Foulard smiled slightly, "It is a good plan except for the last. It is customary for our strategists to protect themselves. There are quite a few officers who will be glad to volunteer for the job in the plane." He rose steadily. "You must go with the President, sir. Good luck."

He started for the door, and the President rose and gripped his hand. "You go with me in the car, General," he ordered.

The general shook his head. "The south attack must be carried through, sir. It is imperative that at least a guard of those men reaches Arlington, also. I think the boys will do that…for me, sir, and for you. But they'll do a better job if I go with them." He laughed, with a little embarrassment. "It's a long time since I've had a chance at action, sir."

He saluted and strode out.

IN fifteen minutes, all preparations were made. Two machine guns were mounted in each of four sedans, one on the left of the rear seat, one on the right in the front. It left room only for two men to lie on the floor in the rear. In the second car, Holme and the President lay side by side. Wentworth took his post at the rear-seat machine gun. Zero hour was six-ten; the plane would attempt to rise at six-fourteen. At six-fifteen, the cars would crash the northern entrance in Pennsylvania. There was no more to the battle plan than that. Those who survived the southern attack, would attempt to reach Arlington in commandeered cars, or in the three automobiles which would attempt to follow them—intended as a decoy.

Wentworth glanced at his watch and his breath sucked in thinly between his teeth. He met the President's confident smile from the floor.

"Zero hour in fifteen seconds," Wentworth said flatly.

The President said quietly, "I'd feel better if I were handling one of the guns."

His last word was drowned in a crashing roll of gunfire, in which rifles and machine guns joined in a crescendo thunder. Wentworth glued his eyes on his watch. Two men were at the doors of the basement garage. They would leap aboard the fourth car, the last of those which would attempt to reach Pennsylvania Avenue.

Abruptly, outside the northern entrance, machine guns began to rattle. Above the uproar, Wentworth lifted his voice. "One minute. Ready at the doors!" Those machine guns, if his plan went right, would be pointed upward at the plane. If they struck swiftly now…Eyes on the watch, Wentworth checked off seconds. "Fifteen seconds!" he cried. *"Open those doors!"*

The doors ripped open. The first car spurted down the short gentle slope toward the tall iron gates and, in its wake, the car, which bore Wentworth and the President of the United States, which bore the hopes of a nation, roared in a desperate race with death!

CHAPTER THIRTEEN
Via Dolorosa

MARINES had fought for the honor of entering the car that would lead the charge. Its men were picked gunners, selected for deadly accuracy, for high courage. Curiously, as the sedans ranged forward, a song rose above the mechanic roar of the guns, above the deep-throated power of the engines, the hymn of the Marine brigade! Men swung the muzzles of machine guns and sang—sweeping the barricades that lined Pennsylvania Avenue.

Wentworth chanced a single quick glance aloft. The autogiro was in the air, fluttering like some giant insect through a hail of upflung lead. Even as he glimpsed it, the machine faltered, began to drift downward and a ragged cheer lifted from the enemy ranks. Wentworth's mouth parted and a mirthless laugh poured forth. He laid his eyes and his gun on the barricades ahead.

Up to this point his plan had worked. It had given them the maximum of surprise. It had won them fifteen seconds to race for the iron gates. Nothing could have gained them more. Holme Guards, in their fury, in the first shock of the surprise, were struggling frantically to yank their machine guns' muzzles from the skies to bear on this new threat. In their haste, they threw caution to the winds and exposed themselves. Wentworth saw the entire crew of one gun scythed down by machine-gun bullets. At another, one man was left to labor over the weapon amid a rain of bullets that seemed unable to harm him. Two guns wiped out, but there were a dozen bearing on this one gate—from across the width of the avenue, and enfiladed from barricades to each side.

The burst of the bombs with which the first car had been supplied tore at the iron gates, left them sagging, but still half upright. Men were screaming there. Two machine guns were hammering at the cars now and rifles blazed at point-blank range. Wentworth saw the leading car swerve in its true course just as it fairly leaped from the earth in a burst of power that hurled it full-speed against the gaping gates!

There was a clang of steel on steel, a shattering crash and the gates were hurled violently from their hinges, tossed into the path of men who charged forward on either side. The car ahead wobbled erratically, its speed cut in half, quartered. It had expended itself in that final burst. Wentworth saw that a dead man lay across the wheel, that even in death his hands tried to do their duty. The Marine machine gunners paid no heed at all. Theirs was the job of handling their weapons and they did it terribly. As the car turned broadside, rolled westward along Pennsylvania as gently as on parade, they manned their weapons and sprayed the barricades from behind. Those Marines were doomed, but they had fought for the privilege of dying thus gloriously for President and country. Wentworth could no longer hear their song, but their lips were moving. It could not last. Ah, God, it could not!

Wentworth was wielding his own machine gun on a loose pivot, whipping it from side to side, hammering down a charge of riflemen. A guard whipped back a grenade, his wide-pulled eyes fixed on the President's car. The muzzle of the machine gun swept in a quarter turn and the man's arm bowed backward the grenade; fell to the ground and burst amid the enemy.

Without a pause, Wentworth's gun blazed at the nearest machine gun, drove the loader and the gunner to bloody death.

The blast that poured from Wentworth's lips was sheer exultation. By the heavens, he could not miss today. He…A slug plucked the uniform cap from his head, dazed him for a split-second. In that moment, he heard the second-machine gun in his car go dead. Only for an instant, then it was hammering again and Wentworth realized that they had made the turn to eastward on Pennsylvania Avenue; that he no longer had a target for his machine gun.

With an oath, Wentworth lifted the heavy machine gun in his arms and heaved it across to the opposite side where the Holme Guard was frantically trying once more to realign its guns. All had been trained in the direction of the White House and now Wentworth was behind the barricades. It was only necessary to lift the guns and swing them about, but tripods hampered them. Wentworth had jerked free of the tripod, rested the smoking hot jacket on the door of the car. The jar of the recoil ran through all his body, taxed his strength to the utmost. But as the car gained speed, his bullets hummed among those disorganized forces.

IT WAS only when the last of that line of trenches swept by that Wentworth dared glance about at his car. He had been aware of movements beside him, of that instant of quiet when the machine gun had faltered. A shout of apprehension shook him. The President was no longer on the floor! Crouched half erect, leaning across the back of the front seat, he manipulated the forward machine gun whose operator sprawled dead behind it. There was a spatter of blood across the President's face, but as he straightened stiffly a smile widened his mouth.

"Hot work, *Spider*," he cried above the engine roar. "But those poor brave men..."

Wentworth flung a glance behind. He saw the last car in line sway erratically, lurch half about in the broad street then charge head-on for the barricades where the last machine guns bore down the avenue; those which alone still periled the fleeing President. No machine guns spoke from that car. The lurch had hurled a dead man to the pavement, but the driver still was in control. Savagely, he rammed the barricade. The bodies of men flew and a machine gun was ground into earth. The driver sprang to one of his own unmanned weapons and for five glorious seconds swept death at the enemy. Then he, too, was dead.

Only two cars were left, racing frantically down the broad stretch of the avenue. Free, the street ahead open to them, they raced for Fourteenth Street—for the sweep to the bridge and Arlington. Wentworth faced front again.

"We're through, sir," he said curtly. "We—"

He stared at the driver. He lolled, half unconscious behind the wheel. With his left hand alone, the Marine was battling to hold the speeding car to the road. Wentworth lunged forward, seized the wheel across his shoulders.

"Move to one side, if you can," he said quietly. "You've done your job."

The man's head rolled limply on his shoulders and he pitched sideways across the body of his dead companion. His foot lifted off the accelerator. Before Wentworth could shout, the President had seized the man and heaved him into the back. Wentworth slid behind the wheel, drove the accelerator to the floor-board and rocketed on screaming tires into Fourteenth Street and southward. He had gained no sight of the battle on the south lawn, but he threw a glance at his watch. Eighteen minutes past six. Eight minutes since the attack to the south had been launched; three since their own charge had begun. How many minutes before the commander of the guard would learn of this crush-out? Before he would guess the object of the sortie? The 'giro was no longer in the sky, but there were other planes, darting, machine-gun armed hawks of death. *They* would guess.

Even as the thought came to Wentworth, he heard the slower, broken firing of a propeller-interrupted gun and bullets gouged through the right side of the car, swept on. He heard the zoom of a soaring motor.

"Holme, damn you!" the President was shouting. "Help me get this machine gun out the back window!"

In the rear-vision mirror, Wentworth had a glimpse of the white-haired President, his face grim beneath the blood stains, wrestling with the heavy weapon. The car behind was blazing away at a diving plane. Wentworth threw his own machine sideways in a sharp skid, cut back again—and heard the zoom of the plane as it swept up again to return to the attack, its motor roaring with thwarted rage.

Wentworth's lips were drawn back from his teeth with futile anger. Nine, ten miles from the Arlington radio station and all the way these hawks would dart and hurl their deadly ammunition! A little way farther, there were trees which would serve to blind them a little, but that straight bridge, open to the skies! They could not dodge forever. Once more the cough of the machine guns heralded the plane's dive and Wentworth jerked the car to the right, kicked the brakes; once more, he had evaded the plane.

"Only one plane?" he called back sharply.

"The other went toward the airport,'" the President called back steadily. "If I could only stop this one! Hold steady, instead of dodging, and I think..."

Wentworth shook his head, zigzagged frantically. The President cried out triumphantly. "He's hit! The car behind us scored! Oh, those brave men!"

The jubilation in his voice was wholly inspiring.

WENTWORTH twisted about, saw the car behind swerve wildly, straighten once, then yaw again. It carried through a lamp post, brought it crushing down on its top, rolled on

A machine gun was pointed upward, spraying the air around the autogiro over the White House!

across the street and slammed head-on into a building. In the wreckage, nothing stirred at all. They had taken the chance Wentworth had not dared to take with the custody of the President in his hands. But, overhead, the plane was faltering in its zoom. Puffs of black smoke burst from beneath the fuselage, then red tongues of flame. Wentworth ground the accelerator to the floor.

Sixty, seventy, seventy-five—the speedometer needle swung upward steadily, wavered at eighty, then crept on. The windshield had long since vanished. The pressure drove Wentworth's breath into his nostrils, half-blinded his unprotected eyes. Grimly, he held it. Impossible to see the speedometer now, but the drone of the engine seemed to shriek at a higher pitch. A slight wide turn made the car sway perilously and the road ahead was winding.

Wentworth set as nearly a straight course as possible, shooting from side to side of the road as he minimized the curves. There was a constant shrill whine of the tires and through the sound the machine gun began to speak again. His shouted query was plucked from his lips by the roaring wind and the answer came back faintly.

"Motorcycle Squad!"

After the other perils, this one seemed slight. No machine guns there. They would carry rifles on their backs, but would be helpless to use them. Revolvers, of course. He heard a shout from the President, glimpsed a motorcycle that swerved and then rolled like a wounded horse. Its driver flew a hundred feet through the air, a dark doomed projectile. A second swerved, tangled with a third and, afterward, the motorcycle pursuit dropped back, but hung on doggedly. Wentworth braked for the whirl into the straight course of the bridge. A quick side-glance showed him a flight of airplanes rising like a flock of fearful birds from the airport.

The car wrenched, wobbled wildly on the curve, straightened out as he threw gas into the engine and the dash across the bridge was on. Far ahead, spidery against the sky, lifted the radio towers of Arlington. Once more, he glanced toward the planes, toward the motorcycles. The cycle squad was gone! Even as he dared a second glance, a line of four automobiles shot the last one from the road and swept on. And, flaunting above their hoods, strapped immovably and high above the roofs, were...were the battle flags of the Marines! *Foulard!* General Foulard had crashed through!

By the heavens, nothing could stop them now! Nothing...Up through the winding roads of the Virginia hills, that slim army of despair fought its way. Two cars were smashed by plane fire, another wrecked by a dropped bomb, but the ambuscade of machine guns took its toll in the air, too, and before that devastating hail of death, the Holme Guard planes drew off and circled faint-heartedly.

WITH only a handful of men left out of the regiment that had guarded the White House, the President was borne into Arlington radio station, and within minutes the operators were laboring to carrying out Wentworth's orders. Wide open, scattered over every waveband in the ether, that powerful station would carry the President's voice to the nation, telling of the horror and death in Washington.

While the President rested, his face calm and determined, the Marines threw their two cars as a barricade across the roadway; they settled their machine guns and rifles. General Foulard's left arm was strapped, broken, to his side. There was a blood-stained bandage around his temples.

"Now we have a radio, sir," he said, "there are some boys with the fleet who would like to join in the fun."

Wentworth smiled slightly. "They're on the way, General. Have been for almost twenty-four hours, but at their best speed they can't arrive before tonight. In about four hours, their planes should be within range, but unless we can reach the people of the country before then—before an hour is out!—it may be too late. Once Holme is elected..."

Wentworth paused and stared at the spirit-broken Holme who had brought this horror upon the nation. His face was without expression, but now and then there was a quiver in his lips. There was no help there. Only one help—the Master must know by now where his puppet was, and it might serve to draw him within range of the *Spider's* guns.

"Ready, sir!" the radio men called. "Ready for the broadcast."

Wentworth caught up the microphone offered. "All stations off the air," he ordered sharply. "All stations off the air. This is the Federal station at Arlington calling. All stations off the air. This is the combined order of the President of the United States and of Senator Roger Holme. The President will speak to you."

He handed the microphone to the President, with a smile.

"The air is yours, sir," he said.

The President said quietly, "My people…"

He said no more than that. Crashing down from the air came a man's voice, enormously magnified by a loud-speaker. "Stop that broadcast," it said, "or I'll tear down the aerials!"

Wentworth darted to a window and stared up into the skies. Circling just above the aerials, a plane droned steadily and it was from that the voice came. Below the plane, two human bodies dangled, strung up by their hands, the bodies of two women.

"Cease that broadcast," the voice ordered again, "or the bodies of these women shall tear down the aerials! Perhaps you will recognize the women, gentlemen? Perhaps not. They are…Ellen Mayfrew and Nita Van Sloan!"

CHAPTER FOURTEEN
"A Man Can Only Die."

WENTWORTH'S hand closed hard and white on the frame of the window, but no sound came from his lips. He was aware that the President had ceased to speak, that General Foulard stood beside him.

"We can't stop," he said harshly. "Hundreds of men have died to win this position. Two more lives added to that toll cannot stop us."

Wentworth's throat closed. He forced out a word hoarsely, "No," he said, "we cannot stop."

It was the President's weary voice which came to him. "Two lives, no. But we cannot broadcast without aerials. Who is that man in the plane?"

Wentworth said, more quietly: "Daniel Borough. He was not assassinated that day at the Capitol, possibly not even wounded. It was a clever subterfuge to mask himself. Nita Van Sloan holds the evidence to convict him if she…if she lives. She knows, too, the whereabouts of Yolanda Blanton's son—a lever to fully open Yolanda's lips!" A hand touched Wentworth's arm hesitantly and he turned to meet the pale, staring face of Roger Holme. For the first time in hours something like intelligence was in his eyes.

"You said…Daniel Borough?" he whispered. "I begin to understand. He built me up from the first for just this. He victimized me…Nita Van Sloan left a message *cave mortuum qui vivit*. Beware the dead who live! Why, that temple of Siva was in Borough's closed house! I knew that place was familiar, but closed up that way…"

"Certainly, Borough!" Wentworth said crisply. "There was a time when I suspected Mayfrew. His suicide seemed unnecessary. But the crooks behind you, Holme, must have found some secret in his past. His conscience would not permit him to keep silent; they would not allow him to speak, so he killed himself to point a path for me to follow…Holme, you have a conscience. At heart, you are a fine man. You would be willing to talk over the radio, if we can…smash this plan of theirs?"

Holme's head was up with something of its former challenge and the deep, ringing timber of old began to creep back into his voice.

"Certainly. But Ellen! God, she told me all this a thousand times and I would not listen. You must save Ellen. I cannot bear the thought of another sacrifice."

Wentworth's lips twitched. God, if only he could save Ellen—and Nita. Sweet Nita.

"I will save them," he said flatly. "General, see that Holme remembers his promise!"

The President's hand closed on Wentworth's shoulder. "What can you do, man?

There isn't any way...Why, the guard is already surrounding this place." The rattle of gunfire outside confirmed his words.

Wentworth laughed and it was the old reckless laughter of daring and courage and strength. "With the help of God, sir, and those brave girls up there..." He swung to the door. The girls dangled by their hands from the cross-brace between the landing wheels, obviously tied there. A dive into the aerials would slice their bodies to ribbons. If the plane were forced down, they would be dragged upon the earth at better than sixty miles an hour to certain death. But the plane had never taken off with them in that position. Plainly, they had been perched on that bar, then shaken off by violent maneuvers. And if they had swung down, perhaps they could swing back...Even as he stared, he saw that one of the girls was attempting to lift her feet up over the bar, the girl in a Holme Auxiliary uniform. And Wentworth's breath caught hard in his throat. Nita! It could only be Nita. If she could accomplish that maneuver...

Wentworth swung about. "Create a diversion of some sort," he said quietly. "Argue with the Master by radio. I'm going up the radio tower."

Foulard caught his arm. "It's certain death, man! You'll be entirely exposed to gunfire."

Wentworth shook his head. "Not entirely. And...a man can only die, General!"

SWIFTLY, Wentworth set to work. He got two fully loaded automatics, swung a rifle across his shoulders by its strap and slipped out of the building. He heard the President's voice remonstrating over the radio, heard a brisk gunfire open up as Foulard furnished a "diversion." Then Wentworth was around the radio shack and at the base of the central tower of the three which bore the aerials far aloft. The guard's encircling movement did not give them a view of this part of the tower yet, but when he got above the roof line...

Wentworth ran swiftly up the ladder and was halfway up the spidery tower before the shouts of men reached him and bullets began to whine. They spanged off the steel framework, which offered a partial protection, and his rapid movement helped, too. He was already panting heavily, sweat streaming down his body as he whiled upward under the heavy load of armament, racing against time, against bullets.

He dared a quick glance at the circling plane, saw it straighten toward him in a dive, heard the machine gun begin to cough. On the cross-bar, Nita had succeeded in getting her knees hooked over the brace and was straining her body upward, handicapped by the bonds that held her wrists. Ellen still swung. Wentworth dared not risk a shot at the plane yet, but he raced—raced upward. Only swift movement could save him. He heard the rattle of machine-gun bullets just below him. His foot flew from a brace and for a moment he thought he had been hit. There was a gouged tear that had ripped half the sole from his shoe. The plane swerved wildly to avoid the tower, zoomed, and the deep, magnified voice boomed out.

"Down!" it ordered. "Down from that tower, or I cut the aerials with those women's bodies!"

Wentworth tore a pair of wire-cutters from his pocket. He was only ten feet below the point at which the pulled aerials were secured. If he could reach that...The plane was circling upward, ranging off from the aerials for the rush that would smash through them at sufficient speed not to endanger the plane.

"Start down at once!" the voice roared.

Wentworth reached the tackle of the aerials, began to fumble with fatigue-stiffened hands. The cutters slipped from his hand and plunged downward. Wentworth whipped out his automatic and laid its muzzle against the cable. The plane was poised like a hawk.

"The last chance!" the voice roared. "Going down?"

Wentworth pulled the trigger. The wire twanged, a few strands cut, but did not part. Above, the Master's plane started its dive. Frantically, Wentworth pulled the trigger. Again…again. He dared not stare upward at the plane, must keep his eyes on the cable. The roar of the motor came on at incredible speed. Ah, damn the cable! Damn the cable! Wentworth fired until the hammer clicked emptily, saw the last strand part as the ship zipped past…

Wentworth scarcely dared to look upward toward the plane. He had heard the *zing* of jerking wires. Had they been broken, or had the tension from the other end…He pulled his eyes heavily upward. The plane was diving again, the machine gun sputtering. Nita was balanced on the bar and she lifted one hand to Wentworth, one hand *free*—as the ship flashed in. Only for a second, then she was bending over Ellen.

The sound that blew from Wentworth's lungs was half laughter, half-shouted defiance. He had been in time, then! Rapidly, he swarmed up the radio mast. Up here near the top, the steel frame-work was closer together, almost solid. It shed the constant hammer of machine-gun bullets. When the ship swept past, he would have a split-second in which he could return the fire, then he must dodge frantically to the other side of the tower before the plane whirled again to the attack.

Precariously, he maneuvered the rifle from its sling, belted it tightly to his upper arm. His lips were hard set. He could not kill the Master. The man must be left free to maneuver the plane to a landing. But he must kill that engine, or he would die and Nita would die and the message would never go out to the people; the fleet would come too late.

● **THE CITY THAT DARED NOT EAT**

Famine stalked the streets of America's greatest metropolis, and those starving multitudes who sat down to eat found only empty plates and a grinning skeleton at the feast! For the underworld, under a criminal **Red Spider**, had slashed the city's life-giving arteries, decreeing that all who opposed their rule must perish. In that heart-breaking world of shrunken bodies and beggared babies crying for milk, Richard Wentworth donned the real Spider's armor of mercy. Never before had he faced such a foe—a crime master who could not only serve out slow death to millions but also make another man's life his own!

**THE SPIDER
THE MASTER OF MEN!**

Don't miss this amazing story of thrilling crime-war, of the *Spider's* greatest fight against the wolves of society! A book-length novel of an epoch-making battle-behind-the-law, complete in the October issue!

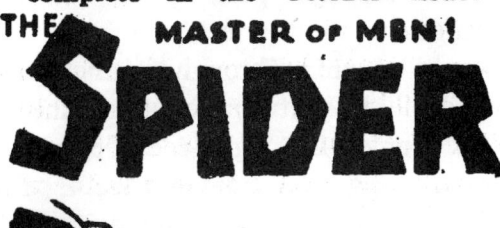

Out September 3

Ten Cents

AS the plane raced closer, Wentworth braced his feet on a cross-strut within ten feet of the top, poked the rifle forward. There was only a fraction of an instant to aim, to calculate the headlong pace of the plane. He squeezed off a shot—and the plane had dodged past the mast, was roaring on, swinging to dive again. No time to reach the other side of the mast. Time only to move halfway about, then to bring up the rifle again.

Words, his own vaunting words, rang through his brain. *A man can only die.* Yes, but his death now meant the death—of a nation! Wentworth saw the machine guns of the plane come in line and, abruptly, thought was gone from his brain. Only one thing remained. There was a motor that he knew as he knew the palm of his hand. He knew just where to hit to smash the ignition system, to force the plane down, and here was a rifle in his hands which had the power to smash it.

The plane was coming in more slowly, pulled upward so that the Master's aim would be surer. Through the thick glass of the windshield, Wentworth could see the florid face of Daniel Borough, see the hate that shrank his lips back from his teeth. Flame blossomed at the muzzles of the twin machine guns. Wentworth scarcely saw it, saw only the motor cowling. He squeezed the trigger of the rifle, manipulated the bolt, fired again. Then a hammer beat at his body. Only his elbow, hooked through the casework, kept him from falling as his feet slipped from their hold. He swung limply, his dimming eyes on the plane. It swerved barely clear of the tower. Nita…She and Ellen were both crouched on the bar now and he heard her shout. He heard her shout…Then the motor was dead! His shot had gone home.

Wentworth laughed faintly. The rifle dangled heavily from its strap about his elbow. He picked it up clumsily and thrust it between steel bars until it caught. Even if he fainted now, the strap would save him from falling. He wondered vaguely how badly he was hit. But he had won…He had won! The plane would be forced down. Those Guardsmen would never stand against the flying wedge of the Marines as they raced to the rescue of the girls. Repair the radio, the President and Holme on the air… Curious, he seemed to be able to hear their voices. He rolled his head, tried to move an arm and found it was bound to his chest. Hell, he was inside the radio shack! And Nita's face was above him and Nita's cool hands upon his forehead.

"Borough?" Wentworth whispered.

Nita smiled. "Quite dead," she whispered. "The first planes from the fleet have been sighted, and…Listen."

"To one man," came the President's timbered voice, "the nation owes its salvation. To a man who chooses to be known as the *Spider*. If we are a whole nation today, his the credit. For such crimes as are against his name, I give him full and free pardon. He is the real…Sword of Justice."

~ THE END ~

Spider Gallery

By FRANKLYN E. HAMILTON

Franklyn E. Hamilton originally created this illustration of The Spider's signet ring for the back cover of *Echoes* #3, the legendary fanzine published by Tom and Ginger Johnson. *Echoes* celebrated its 100th issue a few months ago, and the early issues have several illustrations by Frank, featuring a variety of characters from the pulps and other realted media. Naturally, our big interest is in The Spider, and Frank found several opportunities to render The Master of Men. If you haven't unearthed back issues, just sit back and keep watching *The Spider Gallery* for more terrific artwork.

DEATH SIGNS THE PAYROLL

By FRANK GRUBER

A racket killer's bludgeon fired a man from the Tamer Factory! Douglas March, soldier of hazardous fortune, took his job—and accepted the challenge of a murderer who built his fortune on the misery of human hearts.

CAPTAIN DOUGLAS MARCH sat on the front steps of Mrs. Bayer's boarding house, smoking an after-dinner pipe. Up and down the street other men were sitting on their steps, smoking and reading the evening papers. Women sat out front, too. A group of yelling urchins were playing baseball out on the street.

March enjoyed the peace of these uneventful days in Chicago—But even as he thought about it, the peacefulness of the scene was broken. A black touring car careened around the near corner and came hurtling down the street.

March watched its approach uneasily, for he knew that boys playing ball on the streets were prone to wait too long before dispersing before an automobile.

The car, however, slackened speed as it approached. Its driver tooled it toward the curb, just a few feet from where March was sitting. The tonneau door opened and a man appeared in the doorway. He hesitated there a moment, then suddenly plunged forward. March gasped and came to his feet. He saw the man hit the sidewalk on his face, saw, too, the hands that had propelled him forward.

He sprang down the steps and lunged toward the car. But it was too late. With a roar of gears it shot away. March shot a keen glance at its fast-disappearing rear end, but the license plate was hidden from his sight by the shouting boys, their interest in baseball suddenly diverted. March dropped to his knees beside the man who lay on the sidewalk.

He felt suddenly sick as he saw the blood-soaked hair on the back of the man's head. And the ugly wound.

Yet there was life in the prone figure. As March knelt, the man raised his head a couple of inches and half twisted his face toward March. His mouth worked spasmodically and gasped out the words: *"Couldn't pay... Tamer... Townsend..."*

And then blood spurted from the man's mouth and his face hit the sidewalk. March had seen men die before, in China, Central America, Europe. He rose to his feet.

He became aware of excited chattering all about him. He looked around and saw that a small crowd had already collected and that people were rushing out of buildings on all sides.

The blast of a police whistle split the air. March stepped back, said to everyone in general, "He's dead."

A uniformed policeman burst through the fringe of spectators and almost tripped over the body on the sidewalk.

"Who—what happened?" he gasped.

"A car drove up to the curb," March explained. "This...man...was thrown out. He's dead."

"Who're you?" barked the policeman.

March shrugged. "I live in this house here and happened to be sitting on the steps when the car pulled up."

The cop looked around the circle of faces. A middle-aged, stout woman, nodded her head and said vigorously, "Dot's right. He rooms in my house. Und he's a fine man."

Some alert neighbor had phoned for an ambulance. Its screaming siren heralded its approach.

With the ambulance came a lieutenant of police. The patrolman, already on the scene, relinquished his authority with a sigh of relief.

The dead man was identified by him wailing widow. His name was Tony Kohlman and he lived next door to Mrs. Bayer's boarding house.

"No, he never had no enemies," his widow sobbed.

The ambulance took the body away. The police lingered fifteen or twenty minutes, grilling, asking questions but seemingly paying no attention to the answers. A dozen people, besides March, told the same story. The car had come around the corner, stopped at the curb and Tony Kohlman had been thrown out. Four people had taken the license number of the car.

MARCH told the lieutenant of the dead man's last words. "'Couldn't pay...Tamer...Townsend'."

The lieutenant shook his head. "Gang stuff. The car was probably stolen, but we'll check on it, anyway. But...I never heard of any gangsters named Townsend or Tamer."

And then the police left and life on Cleveland Avenue resumed its usual course. The boys started up their baseball game again. Their elders went back to their front steps, read their newspapers or talked with their neighbors about the "excitement."

BUT March didn't go back to his steps. He went instead into his boarding house and rapped on a door on the second floor. It opened a few inches and a pasty face appeared in it. But it did not smile.

"Uh—hello, Mr. March," said the man

with the pasty face.

"Can I come in, Joe?" March asked.

Joe Becker's face clouded, but March was already pushing his way into the room. Inside, he looked at the open suitcase lying on the bed. "Packing, Joe?" he asked.

"Uh—yes, I'm going out of town for a couple of days. My mother's sick at home."

"Sorry to hear it, Joe." March looked around the room. It was sparsely furnished, much like March's own room. An iron bedstead, a chest of drawers, a rocking chair, a small table. And a radio. That, March knew, didn't come with the room. It was a nice radio as radios went. At least from outward appearance.

"Going to leave your radio behind?" March asked.

Becker's eyes widened and for a moment showed fear. Then he pulled himself together. "Of course, I said I was only going to be gone a couple of days."

March sat on the bed beside the open suitcase. He said, quietly, "Tony Kohlman was a friend of yours, wasn't he, Joe?"

Becker inhaled air sharply. "Yes, but—but…It's too damn bad," he finished lamely.

March looked thoughtfully at Joe Becker. "Listen, Joe," he said. "You heard the noise outside and I saw you looking out of the window. But why didn't you come downstairs? You and Tony Kohlman were such close friends. I saw you together often."

Becker flared up. "I heard someone holler he was dead. What good would it have done me to run downstairs?"

March sighed. "Joe, why was Tony killed?"

Becker backed to the wall. "Why—why, how should I know?"

"I think you know, Joe. Listen, I'm your friend. You can tell me. What are you afraid of?"

Becker's mouth twisted for a moment. Then he half-whispered, "You see, I got a warnin' too."

March leaned forward. "From who?"

"What the hell!" Becker burst out. "If they're gonna give it to me, I can't help it. I'll tell you. It was the Acme Adjustment Agency."

"What's that? A collection agency?"

Becker nodded. "It's this radio. I bought it on time and then I lost my job and couldn't keep up the payments."

"Then why didn't you let them take the radio back?"

"They wouldn't do it. They said I had to pay for it in full."

"How much do you still owe on it?"

"Sixty dollars. It was one-twenty altogether. I paid ten dollars down and five a month."

"I think you got gypped on it," said March. "I doubt if that radio is worth more than sixty dollars."

"You're telling me? I've seen better ones since for forty bucks. But, anyway, the company claimed that I signed an agreement giving them the right to garnishee my wages if I didn't keep up the payments. I worked at the American Tea Company then and when they garnisheed my wages I got fired. A company rule. Lots of companies have 'em. Then when I was out of a job the gyp radio outfit sold my bill to this Acme company. They're the ones that have been after me lately. They were after Kohlman, too."

"Ah," said March. "Now we're getting somewhere. Kohlman bought a radio, too?"

"No, he bought furniture, from the Tish Furniture Company. I don't think he got gypped like I did on this radio but his payments were too stiff and he had a hard time meeting them. Then the company sold his bill to the Acme gang. And they started hounding him…and he had a job with the Tamer Leather Company."

"Tamer?" exclaimed March sharply.

"Yeah, it's a big place over on Townsend Street."

March's forehead wrinkled. Tamer and Townsend. Tony Kohlman had gasped out these two words. Had he merely been worried about his job? Or had his brutal assault something to do with the leather factory?

March questioned Becker further. The latter talked freely once he had got started. The Acme Adjustment Agency apparently specialized in delinquent and hard-to-collect accounts, which some installment houses were no doubt glad to dispose of at a discount, particularly when they had already collected most of the retail value of the merchandise sold. March knew something about installment merchandise, knew that a hundred-dollar piece of furniture seldom cost the dealer more than thirty dollars and that anything they got over that was clear profit. If a furniture company could collect sixty dollars on a hundred-dollar bill and then sell the balance for half-price it was doing a profitable business.

When he had heard the complete story from Becker, March said, "Listen, Joe, I don't know if this Acme outfit had anything to do with Kohlman's death, but I'm going to try to find out and if they did..."

"You'll fix 'em, Captain?" asked Becker, eagerly. "If anyone can do it, you can. These cops..."

"I'm going to try my best," March promised. "But in the meantime, Joe, to play safe, I think it would be best if you really left town for a few days."

Joe Becker left Mrs. Bayer's boarding house a half hour later, by the rear door. And March took over Becker's room.

As he saw it, there would be a lot to do now.

IN THE morning he put on one of Joe Becker's old suits. Unshaved and walking with a slouch, he could pass readily enough for a factory hand.

The address of the Acme Adjustment Agency was given as Room 1412, Pelard Building. When March called there he was chagrined to find it merely a mailing address concern, presided over by a youthful Armenian.

The Armenian drove a hard bargain with March. It cost the latter ten dollars to get the information he wanted.

"All I do is readdress the mail to Ninety eight Wells Street," he said.

March walked over to 98 Wells Street. His suspicions about the Acme Adjustment Agency were growing and they became even more concrete when he discovered the office on the eighth floor of 98 Wells Street to be locked.

He found a locksmith at Randolph and Wells and for $1.50 purchased five keys. Four were unnecessary, for the first one unlocked the door of the collection agency.

March went into the office, locked the door on the inside and switched on the electric lights. The place was sparsely furnished. There was merely a battered desk, a card file and a couple of chairs.

March went through the desk, found that it contained only stationery bearing the name and mailing address of the Acme Adjustment Agency.

He attacked the card index. There were about five hundred cards. He ran over the B's and found a card for Joe Becker. Typed on it was the name and address of Joe Becker and a cryptic notation:

$60.—1—2—3. S. A. next.

S. A. That probably meant "strong arm".

There was no card for Tony Kohlman. Which was strange, for Becker had assured March that this same outfit had been after Kohlman...But perhaps it wasn't so strange. They had "collected" from Kohlman and removed his card from the file. He was not 'active' now.

There wasn't a single thing in the office by which March could identify an individual with the Acme Adjustment Agency. The owners of the agency, it seemed, preferred to remain incognito.

He was about to leave the office when he saw the knife lying on the desk. It was a queer knife. It had a round wooden handle and a crescent-shaped blade about eight inches long. But the blade was curved downwards, toward the cutting edge instead of away from it as in most knives. And instead of being pointed the blade was cut off squarely.

March frowned as he stared at the knife. It was not a common type, but not an uncommon type either. He raised the thing to his nostrils and caught the faint odor of...leather.

Yes, of course. This was a leather knife. Shoe repair men used it. So did workers in leather factories. And someone in the Acme Adjustment Agency used it to open envelopes.

Tony Kohlman had worked in a leather factory. The trail to it was growing strong. And...there should be a vacancy at the leather factory.

March put the knife back on the desk and left the office. He caught a Clybourn Street car outside and rode in it to Division and Crosby. He left the car there, walked two blocks to Townsend Street and the Tamer Leather factory.

The company had a surprisingly small office force, merely a girl and a cold-faced man of about forty-five. March guessed that the company had its main office downtown.

"Need any help, Mister?" March asked.

"No," the cold-faced man said. "We're full up."

"Sure, mister?" persisted March. "I—uh—thought maybe there'd be an opening on account of...of that fella that was bumped off yesterday."

The office man sat erect. "So you heard about that and thought you'd hurry over and get his job, huh?" He added something under his breath that sounded like "buzzard", but March pretended not to hear.

"Yeah," the man went on. "Maybe we do need a man. I'll find out." He picked up his phone, pushed an electric button and waited. March heard a horn blow out in the factory, two long and three short blasts. It was a call system used in factories for locating foremen who usually couldn't hear phone bells because of the noise of machinery.

After a moment the office man spoke into the telephone. "Hello, Johnny? George Reese. Do you need a man? Yeah thought you would. All right, I'll send him up."

He hung up the phone and said to March: "Climb up to the third floor and ask for Johnny Carson. I guess he can put you on."

March's face lit up. "Thanks, mister." He left the office and climbed the concrete stairs to the third floor. He entered into a babel of noise.

PULLEYS whined, machines stamped, roared and banged. Factory hands, both men and women, worked at benches and machines. The smell of leather was strong and pungent in March's nostrils. He didn't like it...Neither did these workers perhaps, but they had to put up with it.

"Where's Carson, the foreman?" March asked a strapping young man who wore a blue shop apron.

The man shook his head, roared, "What?"

March roared back: "Carson, the foreman!"

"He's back in the counter department." The man amplified his instructions by pointing to the rear of the building. March made his way through machines and barrels and workers to the rear of the building. The noise was less violent back here. Finally, in a long, narrow room, shut off from the main room by row upon row of stacked wooden barrels, he found an athletic-looking man of middle age. He wore a tan canvas shop coat. The coat distinguished him from the ordinary workers who wore merely aprons and March guessed that he was the foreman.

"Mr. Carson?" March asked. "Mr. Reese said you had a job."

The foreman looked at March. "Yeah, I got a job," he said. "But I don't know whether you want it. It only pays $18.50 a week."

March simulated eagerness. "That's all right. I need a job bad. I been out of work a long time."

"Yeah? Well, if I put you on will you stick until you find another job?" The foreman asked the question disarmingly. March almost stumbled into the trap but caught himself in time.

"No, I'll stick here I ain't much for changin' jobs. I'm a steady worker. Just try me out, mister. You'll see."

The foreman shrugged. "Well, you don't look much like a factory hand, but I'll give you a trial. When can you start to work?"

"Right now!"

Carson turned away. "Oh, Hugo!" he yelled at the top of his voice.

A fifty-foot bench, divided into sections, stretched along the outer wall. At each section, save one, a man sat on a high stool and sorted leather counters, hard upright supports for the heels of shoes.

A grizzled old man with long white mustaches left one of the sections along the bench and waddled up. "Here's a new man for you, Hugo," Carson said and walked off into the noisy section of the shop.

"I'm Hugo Gonsser, the straw boss." the old fellow said. "C'mon, I put you to work." He led the way to one of the vacant sections of the bench. It was piled high with leather counters, thrown on the bench.

The first thing March saw was a leather knife on the bench. A duplicate of the one he had seen at the Acme Adjustment Agency. His eyes lit up.

"We gotta sort these," Hugo explained. "They're all two—M-O-X-O's, but we got to sort them for heavy, medium and rejects. And trim those that got ridges or been squeezed out of shape by the moulding machine. Like this."

He picked up a moulded counter with his right hand, flipped it into the palm of his left and squeezed it expertly with both hands. "Feel this," he said then. "It's a heavy."

March felt it. "And what's a medium?"

Hugo rummaged through the pile, his expert eyes picking out a counter. He tested it. "This is medium," he said.

March felt the counter and shook his head. The difference between a medium and heavy was infinitesimal. "They all feel alike to me," he told the straw boss.

"But they ain't...You'll get the hang of it, soon. Anyway, they're six and a half iron and they're supposed to be heavies. So if there's one you ain't sure about, put it in the heavies."

March chuckled. "I get it, but—what does six and a half iron mean?"

"That's the thickness of the leather. It's measured by irons when it's flat. You know, there's thirty-six irons to an inch."

March hadn't known. He had never heard of an "iron" as a unit of measurement. The thing began to intrigue him. "And what does two—M-O-X-O mean?"

Hugo explained. "The two means second grade, the first grades ain't got glue in 'em. The M stands for men's and the O-X for oxfords. And the last O is the size. Double O is the biggest size. They run double O, O, one, two, all the way to seven, which're for the little kids. Get it: second grade, men's oxfords, size O."

Hugo instructed March further. He showed him how to telescope four counters, then four more and finally turn over one bunch of four and push it into the upright four, making a compact pile, containing eight counters, that was easy to handle. The bunches of eight were piled along the board partition and when there were enough stacked into barrels, stood upright in layers.

Hugo was a garrulous old fellow. "You're lucky to get in my department," he said. "It's the softest work in the place."

"Yeah, but doesn't it get monotonous?"

Hugo was puzzled by the word. "Mono...to...?"

"Tiresome."

Hugo's eyes lit up. "Yeah, sure, but when you git sleepy you can stand up awhile. You won't get that way though...'cause you're the new man and you gotta help pile up the barrels now and then."

He jerked his head toward the rows of barrels behind the drying racks. March grimaced.

"Those barrels look heavy. How do you stack them up four-high?"

"With an elevator. You and Sam'll pile 'em up. You'll see."

Hugo talked volubly about himself, but finally left March to work alone. March climbed up on the high stool and sorted counters for ten minutes in silence. Then a roly-poly German at the bench on March's left spoke to him.

"How you like de chob?"

March shrugged. "A job's a job these days. I been out of work a long time. I'm lucky to get this one…although I hear the fellow who had it before me wasn't so lucky."

The German turned abruptly to his work. March waited a minute, then said, "This *is* the bench that fellow who got knocked off worked at, isn't it? Huh."

There was a strained silence for a moment, then the roly-poly man replied in a low voice, "Yah."

"What sort of a fellow was he?" March persisted.

The German did not answer. March waited awhile, then turned to the man at his right, a young Italian of about twenty or so. "I hear the guy who worked at this bench got knocked off yesterday."

The Italian grinned in a sickly way. "Yeah, I read about it in the papers. S'too bad."

March did not press him further, for he too seemed reluctant to talk about Tony Kohlman.

HUGO returned with a small pad of paper. "Gimme your name and address. I got to turn it in for the payroll."

"Joe Becker's the name," March replied. He added the address. Hugo noted it carefully and departed.

March sorted counters. His back began to ache after a while and he stood up, shifting from foot to foot. Then he sat down on the stool again. After an hour the work seemed unbearable. He left his bench to get a drink of water at the fountain behind the barrels.

When it seemed that he could stand it no longer, the bell finally rang for lunch. Everyone at the long bench stopped work and scurried for the lockers. They brought out their lunches, hurried to their benches and began eating as if their lives depended on wolfing down as quickly as possible.

March shrugged, and ploughing through the myriad of machines in the front part of the shop, left the building. In a restaurant a block away, on Larrabee Street, he caught a quick snack.

At twelve-thirty he was back sorting counters. The afternoon was a nightmare. This was the first day in his life he had ever worked in a factory. At the age of eighteen he was flying airplanes. And at nineteen he was in a war. By the time he had reached twenty-five the newspapers were printing stories about Captain Douglas March, the famous soldier of fortune. He was in Chicago now convalescing from a stubborn wound received in the Gran Chaco a year ago. He'd been taking things easy in Chicago.

Until recently.

And then through circumstances he'd been impressed by the apparent helplessness of the average people around him. For most of his life March had traveled around the world, getting involved in trouble and fighting the fight of the underdog. And then, in Chicago, he'd learned that there were just as many oppressed people as he could find abroad; persons exploited not by governments, but by unscrupulous individuals.

And March had taken up the battle for them. He had entered into the Tony Kohlman thing without hesitation merely because he'd suspected that Tony Kohlman was only one of thousands of people being exploited, harassed and menaced by vicious racketeers.

Strong-arm collection agencies. The Acme Adjustment Agency was only one of many. But this particular one had stepped across the line, had committed murder. And March was determined to bring them to justice. If working at a tedious factory job meant furthering his work, March was willing to do it, no matter how much he detested the work.

But nothing happened that day. March worked at his bench, sorting counters. He tried to talk to his fellow workers, but none would talk about Tony Kohlman. And finally, at five o'clock March had to return to Mrs. Bayer's boarding house with a feeling that he was up against a blank wall. He'd learned some things at the office of the Acme Adjustment Agency. But he hadn't learned enough. There was now a lot more to do.

March had his supper and for an hour afterwards walked the streets. Finally he went into a large drugstore on North Avenue. "I'm an amateur chemist," he told the pharmacist in the prescription department. "I'm wondering if there are any chemicals that would make a very strong stain on the hands that would be hard to remove."

"Sure," replied the pharmacist. "I got some powdered permanganate of potassium on my hands the other day and it was two days before I could get the stain off. I tried everything, too, but the only thing that I found would do the job was oxalic acid."

March talked with the pharmacist for a few minutes, then left the store with a small purchase. In his room at Mrs. Bayer's house, he wrote a letter making it purposely illiterate. It was to the Acme Adjustment Agency and read:

```
Gentlemen:
    Please do not annoy me any more
about that phoney bill you claim I
owe you. I did not buy the radio
from you. And anyway I can get a
better radio for less than the
money you claim I still owe on it.
If you want the radio come and get
it. But I refuse to pay the sixty
dollars.
         Yours truly,
             Joseph Becker
```

A half hour later he mailed the letter.

MARCH was at the Tamer Leather Company at seven-thirty the next morning. He sorted counters until nine o'clock. And then he received a surprising interruption. Reese, the timekeeper, came up to his bench and leaned against it.

"Listen, Becker," he said, "a skip tracer from some collection outfit was just down in the office. Says he has a bill against you and unless you start making payments on it right away, he's going to garnishee your wages. Get it?"

March's face showed amazement that was not simulated. "How the devil did he find out where I was working?"

"How should I know?" snapped Reese. "These skip tracers are damn good though. They sometimes follow a man for days. Well...what are you going to do about it? You know, the company doesn't stand for garnishees. You get your pay garnisheed and you're fired."

"But I don't owe the money to that outfit," protested March. "They bought the claim from the radio store. And I'm perfectly willing to have 'em take back their damn radio."

Reese shook his head. "You're just like all the suckers. You don't look at what you sign. Half the sales contracts the installment houses have state very clearly that the companies do not have to take back their merchandise. The buyer also signs away his right to trial and agrees to pay costs of tracing him in event he skips. The skip tracer that was here said it cost them fifty dollars to find you."

"You mean they're going to add that to the bill?" yelped March.

"Of course—and you better make some arrangements to pay it!"

"I won't!" exclaimed March. "I'll go to the District Attorney's office. This Acme outfit are a bunch of crooks—and worse. I know enough about them to..." He suddenly shut up.

Reese looked at him curiously. "It's your funeral, not mine," he said and walked off.

Ten minutes later Hugo, the straw boss, waddled up to March's bench. "All right, Joe," he said, "You can get your barrel training now."

Sam Salamo, was a stocky, swarthy man of about thirty. "And don't call me salami," he warned March, when Hugo introduced him. He led March to the rear of the stacked barrels. About thirty burlap-covered barrels stood around on the floor. "Here they are," he said. "You'll be sweating by the time we get them all stacked up."

The weights of the different barrels was stenciled on the sides. They weighed from about a hundred and eighty to over two hundred. It seemed that they had to be piled up throughout the various rows of barrels, according to size of the contents.

Sam and March lifted the barrels to a height of two. But when they had to stack them up three and four high, the "elevator" was used. This stood about ten feet high, operated by a cable being wound on a drum. A crank shoved over a squared bar raised the platform on which the barrel and one of the men ascended. A brake was utilized to lower the elevator.

"I usually ride the platform," Sam Salamo said, "but I ain't goin' to take no chances with a greenhorn. The damn handle comes out once in a while."

March had already wondered about that. There was no cotter pin to hold the handle on the squared bar. If the man turning the crank accidentally pulled outwards the crank would come off...and the elevator would drop.

"How often does that happen?" he asked Sam.

"Not often. Last time was two—three months ago."

"What happened...when it fell?"

"The guy was lucky. He only got a busted leg."

March snorted. "*Only* a busted leg. Well, pardner...be damned careful with that crank."

He maneuvered a barrel on to the platform. Sam spat on his hands, braced himself and began turning the crank. March stepped on to the platform containing the barrel as it rose to knee height. There was nothing for him to hold himself...except the barrel, and if the platform dropped out from underneath him, his purchase on a barrel would be a disadvantage.

There was, however, a cross arm on top of the elevator. When it was raised to the height of four barrels March could hang on to that.

Sam stopped turning the crank and applied the brake to the drum. March maneuvered the barrel off the platform on top of another in the stack. It was tricky work and he had to heave and tug to get the barrel on straight so that the cylindrical bottom rested squarely on the top hoop of the barrel underneath.

Sam loosened the brake and the elevator descended swiftly. He braked it to a stop a few inches from the bottom.

Sam leaned against the elevator and looked curiously at March. "I s'pose you ran up a lot of bills while you were outta work, huh?"

"A few," March replied. "But they don't worry me."

"No? Maybe you'll find out different one of these days. I know a collection agency that was after a guy."

"You mean Tony Kohlman?"

"Look," said Sam. "Let's pile up some barrels, huh?"

He maneuvered a barrel onto the platform, then stepped on it. Sam began winding the crank and March wondered suddenly if he had been talking too freely.

He had. When he was near the top, the platform and barrel suddenly dropped away under March. March, sensing something about to happen, had prudently reached out his hands for the cross-bar and he instinctively lunged for it when the platform was whisked out from under him. He caught it and hung there while the platform and barrel hit bottom with a crash that shook the entire factory floor.

March let go his hold on the crosspiece and dropped to the floor.

"It wasn't my fault!" yelped Sam.

He started to back away down the aisle. March squeezed around the elevator and started after Sam. The squat man let out a howl and burst into flight. He caught up to Sam Salamo at the first floor. He caught him by an arm and heaved to a stop.

Then the office door burst open and Steele, the time-keeper, popped out.

"I just got fired," said March, "so I was coming in to get my pay. Sam's, too. He's quitting."

"What the hell you talking about?" barked Steele. "*Your* pay's been garnisheed and Sam...Sam ain't quitting."

"All right. You got my letter, didn't you?"

"What are you talking about?"

March sighed. "So you're going to try denying that you own and operate the Acme Adjustment Agency. You're going to stick to the story that a skip-tracer followed me here?"

"I never even heard of this Acme."

March reached out suddenly and caught hold of Steele's left wrist. He jerked it out of the man's pocket. "Then why the hell are your hands all stained brown? You spilled iodine on them, did you? That's permanganate of potassium and there's only one thing'll take it off. I dusted my letter, that I wrote to you, with the stuff. The moisture in your skin dissolved it and you haven't been able to get it off. When you're in jail, Steele, try using some oxalic acid on it."

Steele brought his right hand out of his pocket and March suddenly let go of the man's left hand and leaped back. There was a wicked-looking leather knife in Steele's hand. He was ready to strike.

"All right, copper," Steele gritted. "You asked for it. You're the only one who knows. No one has even seen me go into the building where I get my mail."

"Sam gets it for you every morning?" asked March. "And he helps you with the strong-arm stuff in the evening?"

Sam Salamo began growling deep in his throat and started moving to get behind March. March let him move a few feet, then suddenly lunged sidewards at him. His fist shot out in a sweeping hook and he struck Steele's henchman a powerful blow on the side of the head. The blow knocked Sam backwards…

The scream startled March. It came from Steele. Sam staggered away from in front of Steele and then March saw the knife in Steele's throat.

The thing had been entirely accidental. When Sam had been knocked against him Steele had instinctively thrown up his forearm to ward him off…and the knife had been turned inwards. The force of Sam's body had hit his forearm and the knife had done the rest.

Steele collapsed to the concrete floor.

March dropped his hand on Sam's shoulder. There was no fight left in the man.

March heaved a tremendous sigh. Avenging Tony Kohlman wouldn't make Kohlman's widow feel any better…but at any rate there would be no other widows because of the Acme Adjustment Agency. And about five hundred people throughout the city would have more money for their families. They would probably never know, and would never ask, why the belligerent collection company no longer bothered them.

SPIDER™ POSTER!

SECRET CITY OF CRIME Poster Magnificent! A striking recreation from *Secret City of Crime* —stunning artwork by Raphael DeSoto, framed by a striking red border with the Pulp Adventures logo! Hang it in your office or dormitory— and watch passerbys become ensnared in The Spider's web! (priority shipping included) **$10.00**

MASTER OF MEN Buttons
Unfortunate badguys wear The Spider's crimson seal on their brow—but you can wear his triumphant logo on your lapel! "The Spider, Master of Men!"—the striking red and yellow logo bordered in black. **$2.00**
(Shipping included with other purchases, otherwise please add $1.00 shipping.)

THRILL TO THESE EARLIER ADVENTURES IN PULP ADVENTURES, INC.'S *SPIDER* SERIES!
#12 Reign of the Silver Terror
#44 The Devil's Pawnbroker
#45 Voyage of the Coffin Ship
#46 The Man Who Ruled in Hell
#47 Slaves of the Black Monarch
#48 Machine Guns Over the White House
$10.00 plus $1.90 shipping per issue —
* Back issues are in limited supply — order now!

ORDER FROM: **Pulp Adventures**

P.O. Box 64,
Bordentown, NJ 08505
(609) 291-5050 (After 12 Noon)
Email: pulpress@aol.com
http://members.aol.com/pulpress/index.html

THE SPIDER MASTER OF MEN! CHECKLIST

Title in **boldface** indicates edition from Pulp Adventures, Inc.

1	The Spider Strikes	Oct 1933
2	The Wheel of Death	Nov 1933
3	Wings of the Black Death	Dec 1933
4	City of Flaming Shadows	Jan 1934
5	Empire of Doom	Feb 1934
6	The Citadel of Hell	Mar 1934
7	Serpent of Destruction	Apr 1934
8	The Mad Horde	May 1934
9	Satan's Death Blast	Jun 1934
10	The Corpse Cargo	July 1934
11	Prince of the Red Looters	Aug 1934
12	**Reign of the Silver Terror**	Sep 1934
13	Builders of the Black Empire	Oct 1934
14	Death's Crimson Juggernaut	Nov 1934
15	The Red Death Rain	Dec 1934
16	The City Destroyer	Jan 1935
17	The Pain Emperor	Feb 1935
18	The Flame Master	Mar 1935
19	Slaves of the Crime Master	Apr 1935
20	Reign of the Death Fiddler	May 1935
21	Hordes of the Red Butcher	Jun 1935
22	Dragon Lord of the Underworld	Jul 1935
23	Master of the Death-Madness	Aug 1935
24	King of the Red Killers	Sep 1935
25	Overlord of the Damned	Oct 1935
26	Death Reign of the Vampire King	Nov 1935
27	Emperor of the Yellow Death	Dec 1935
28	The Mayor of Hell	Jan 1936
29	Slaves of the Murder Syndicate	Feb 1936
30	Green Globes of Death	Mar 1936
31	The Cholera King	Apr 1936
32	Slaves of the Dragon	May 1936
33	Legions of Madness	Jun 1936
34	Laboratory of the Damned	Jul 1936
35	Satan's Sightless Legions	Aug 1936
36	The Coming of Terror	Sep 1936
37	The Devil's Death Dwarfs	Oct 1936
38	City of Dreadful Night	Nov 1936
39	Reign of the Snake Men	Dec 1936
40	Dictator of the Damned	Jan 1937
41	The Milltown Massacres	Feb 1937
42	Satan's Workshop	Mar 1937
43	Scourge of the Yellow Fangs	Apr 1937
44	**The Devil's Pawnbroker**	May 1937
45	**Voyage of the Coffin Ship**	Jun 1937
46	**The Man Who Ruled in Hell**	July 1937
47	**Slaves of the Black Monarch**	Aug 1937
48	**Machine Guns Over the White House**	Sep 1937
49	The City That Dared Not Eat	Oct 1937
50	Master of the Flaming Horde	Nov 1937
51	Satan's Switchboard	Dec 1937
52	Legions of the Accursed Light	Jan 1938
53	The City of Lost Men	Feb 1938
54	The Grey Horde Creeps	Mar 1938
55	City of Whispering Death	Apr 1938
56	When Thousands Slept in Hell	May 1938
57	Satan's Shackles	Jun 1938
58	The Emperor From Hell	Jul 1938
59	The Devil's Candlesticks	Aug 1938
60	The City That Paid to Die	Sep 1938
61	The Spider At Bay	Oct 1938
62	Scourge of the Black Legions	Nov 1938
63	The Withering Death	Dec 1938
64	Claws of the Golden Dragon	Jan 1939
65	The Song of Death	Feb 1939
66	The Silver Death Reign	Mar 1939
67	Blight of the Blazing Eye	Apr 1939
68	King of the Fleshless Legion	May 1939
69	Rule of the Monster Men	Jun 1939
70	The Spider and the Slaves of Hell	Jul 1939
71	The Spider and the Fire God	Aug 1939
72	The Corpse Broker	Sep 1939
73	The Spider and the Eyeless Legions	Oct 1939
74	The Spider and the Faceless One	Nov 1939
75	Satan's Murder Machine	Dec 1939
76	The Spider and the Pain Master	Jan 1940
77	Hell's Sales Manager	Feb 1940
78	Slaves of the Laughing Death	Mar 1940
79	The Man From Hell	Apr 1940
80	The Spider and the War Emperor	May 1940
81	Judgement of the Damned	Jun 1940
82	Dictator's Death Merchants	Jul 1940
83	Pirates From Hell	Aug 1940
84	Master of the Night Demons	Sep 1940
85	The Council of Evil	Oct 1940
86	The Spider and His Hobo Army	Nov 1940
87	The Spider and the Jewels of Hell	Dec 1940
88	Harbor of the Nameless Dead	Jan 1941
89	The Spider and the Slave Doctor	Feb 1941
90	The Spider and the Sons of Satan	Mar 1941
91	Slaves of the Burning Blade	Apr 1941
92	The Devil's Paymaster	May 1941
93	The Benevolent Order of Death	Jun 1941
94	Murder's Black Prince	Jul 1941
95	The Spider and the Scarlet Surgeon	Aug 1941
96	The Spider and the Deathless One	Sep 1941
97	Satan's Seven Swordsmen	Oct 1941
98	Volunteer Corpse Brigade	Nov 1941
99	The Crime Laboratory	Dec 1941
100	Death and The Spider	Jan 1942
101	Murder's Legionaires	Feb 1942
102	The Gentleman From Hell	Mar 1942
103	Slaves of the Ring	Apr 1942
104	The Spider and the Death Piper	May 1942
105	Revolt of the Underworld	Jun 1942
106	Return of the Rackets King	Jul 1942
107	Fangs of the Dragon	Aug 1942
108	Hell Rolls On the Highway	Sep 1942
109	Army of the Damned	Oct 1942
110	Zara: Master of the Damned	Nov 1942
111	The Spider and the Flame King	Dec 1942
112	The Howling Death	Jan 1943
113	Secret City of Crime	Feb 1943
114	Recruit for the Spider Legion	Mar 1943
115	The Spider and the Man From Hell	Apr 1943
116	The Criminal Horde	Aug 1943
117	The Spider and Hell's Factory	Sep 1943
118	When Satan Came to Town	Oct 1943
119	Slaughter, Inc.	1978/1997

THANKS!!!

... for making THE SPIDER™ and PULP ADVENTURES™ the successes of 1998! Get ready for a *new* year of informative articles and hair-raising thrills!

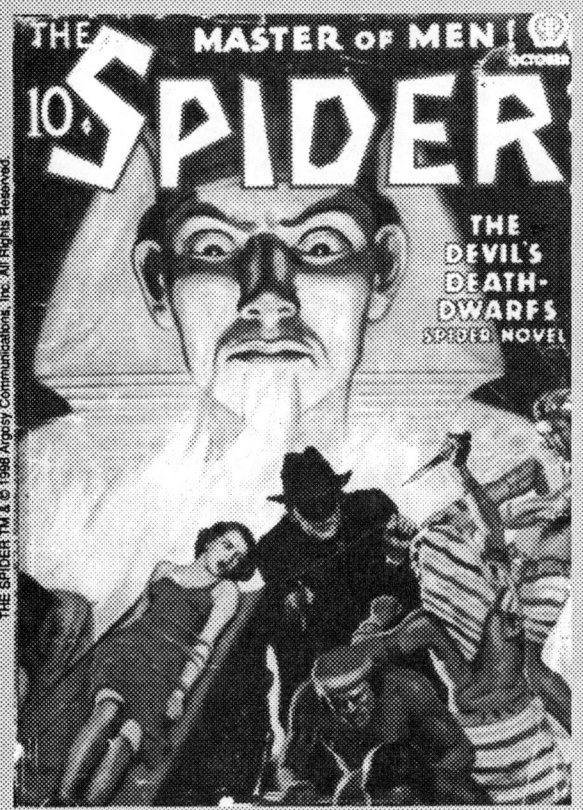

FOR THE FIRST TIME ANYWHERE, "THE LIVING PHARAOH" MINI-SERIES IS BACK IN PRINT!

The Pharaoh and Issoris — two villains so malevolent that it took *four* issues to defeat them! Read The Master of Men's™ epic battle with the Man From the East, and two other startling adventures! Each issue features "Spider Gallery," stunning artwork by Franklyn E. Hamilton, and "The Web," introductions written by illustrious Spider fans like Will Murray, Gahan Wilson, Mark Wheatley, Don Hutchison, and others!

- #21 Hordes of the Red Butcher
- #36 The Coming of the Terror
- #37 The Devil's Death Dwarfs
- #38 City of Dreadful Night
- #39 Reign of the Snake Men
- #85 The Council of Evil

$10.00 plus $1.90 shipping per issue

YOU WILL THRILL TO THESE EARLIER ADVENTURES IN PULP ADVENTURES, INC.'S *SPIDER* SERIES!

- #12 Reign of the Silver Terror
- #44 The Devil's Pawnbroker
- #45 Voyage of the Coffin Ship
- #46 The Man Who Ruled in Hell
- #47 Slaves of the Black Monarch
- #48 Machine Guns Over the White House

* Back issues are in limited supply — order now!

The leading journal for pulp fiction & fact!

Since 1992, Pulp Adventures™ has brought readers articles on the pulp magazines and their modern counterparts. Past interviews have profiled *Shadow* illustrator Michael Kaluta and *Darkman* director Sam Raimi, with classic essays on writing by Walter Gibson and Norvell Page. Every issue is jammed with articles and classic fiction — Pulp Adventures is must-have reading for all pulp fans!

Issues #11 and #12 now on sale
$4.00 each (ppd)
Issue #7 in short supply — $3.00 (ppd.)
Four-issue subscriptions are $16.00

Pulp Adventures, Inc.
P.O. Box 64,
Bordentown, NJ 08505
(609) 291-5050
(Phone/Fax after 12 Noon)
Email: pulpress@aol.com
http://members.aol.com/pulpress/index.html

ORDER FROM:

Checks or Money orders payable to
PULP ADVENTURES, INC.
We accept credit card orders

Adventure House

PRESENTS

Excitement...
Suspense...
AND, BEST OF ALL...
PULPS!!

Order PULP CATALOG #17 for our latest offerings:

- **PULP MAGAZINES**
- Pulp Reprints
- Pulp Cover photographs
- Pulp T-shirts
- Pulp wall-hangings
- Pulp CD-ROMs

ALSO

Our Winning Line-Up of CLASSIC FICTION continues *with*

HIGH ADVENTURE
The King of Pulp Reprints!!
~ *Inquire about our other titles* ~

ADVENTUE HOUSE
914 Laredo Road
Silver Spring, MD 20901
Phone/Fax: (301) 754-1589
http://www.adventurehouse.com/index.htm

SCARLET RIDERS

Edited with an Introduction by Don Hutchison

Action-Packed Mountie Stories from the Fabulous Pulps!

- Includes an unpublished *Silver Corporal* story by *Doc Savage* creator Lester Dent!
- a portfolio of cover art from the original pulp fiction magazines!
- Don Hutchison's first book on the pulp fiction era, *The Great Pulp Heroes*, is now in its 2nd printing!

During the 1920s through the 1940s, tales featuring the rugged Mounties maintaining the law of the untamed North were so popular that a number of authors built careers specializing in their exploits. This is a generous collection of such stories, as flamboyant and red-blooded as the publications in which they first appeared.

History/Literature
ISBN 0-88962-647-2
220 pages, 6x9 PB
$18.95 CAN $14.00 US

ORDER FORM

NAME: _____
ADDRESS: _____ CITY: _____
PROV/STATE: _____ COUNTRY: _____ POSTAL CODE/ZIP: _____
Cost per copy: $14.00 + $2.00 Shipping, Number of copies: _____
Amount enclosed: _____ Payment by cheque( ) payable to Mosaic Press, Visa( )
Mastercard( ) Amex( ) Card Number: _____ Expiry _____

• Canadian orders, add 7% GST

SIGNATURE: _____

RETURN TO: MOSAIC PRESS: 85 RIVER ROCK DRIVE, SUITE 202, BUFFALO, NY, 14207 OR
MOSAIC PRESS: 1252 SPEERS RD, UNITS 1 & 2, OAKVILLE, ON, L6L 5N9, CANADA
PH/FAX 800-387-8992

COMING IN FEBRUARY 1999 ...

... From Pulp Adventures, Inc. ™*

TM & ©1998 Argosy Communications, Inc. All Rights Reserved.
* TM & ©1998 Pulp Adventures Press. All Rights Reserved.